The ECLECTIC

The Life And Times of
Dr. Wallace W. Wheat

The ECLECTIC

The Life And Times of Dr. Wallace W. Wheat

LAURA Z. CLAVIO

Eclectic Institute
Sandy, Oregon

Eclectic Medical Publications
36350 SE Industrial Way
Sandy, Oregon 97055

ISBN # 978-1-888483-17-8 paperback
Library of Congress Control Number: 2013945252

Production by Fourth Lloyd Productions, LLC
Book and cover design by Richard Stodart

Cover photo of Wallace W. Wheat Courtesy of
Galloway Photo and the Parke County Historical Society
Printed in the USA.

Warning: Some of the botanicals illustrated in this book are considered poisonous and some herbal cures should not be administered except by physicians. These plants were used as medicinal preparations by professional pharmacists and physicians. The author takes no responsibility for the use or misuse of any medicinal substances or medical treatments mentioned in this book. Please consult a qualified expert in botanical medicine or your physician for further information. Botanicals used as medicine should be scrutinized for side effects and drugs interactions with any pharmaceuticals you ingest before adding them to your diet.

Sales outlets include: Eclectic Medical Publications, Ingram Book Distributors in the US supplying independent booksellers, Amazon.com, Baker and Taylor, Barnes and Noble. In the UK and Europe, library and bookseller outlets include but are not limited to: Ingram International, Amazon.co.uk, Bertrams, Coutts.

To James D. Clavio, Jr.,
who taught me to appreciate
both history and medicine.

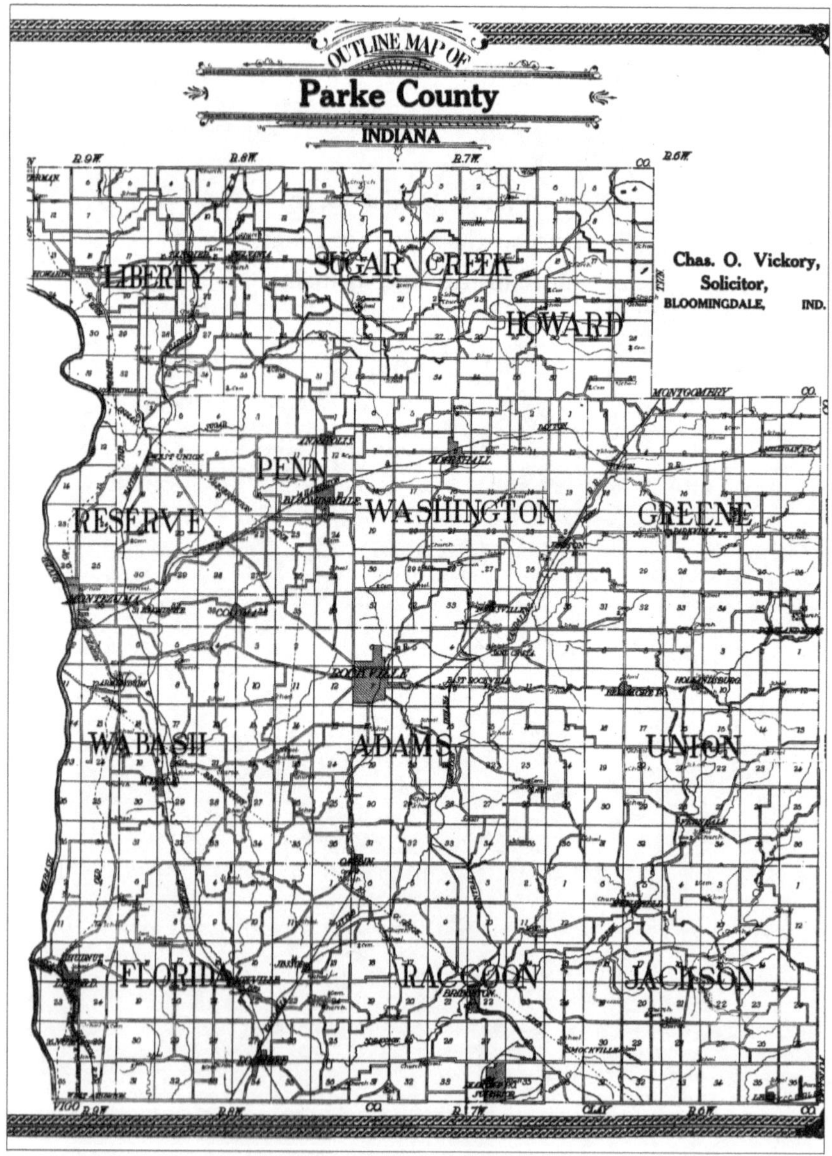

Parke County Indiana map.

This delightful biographical novel tells the life and times of Dr. Wallace Wheat who belonged to the so-called *eclectic* school of medicine, sometimes referred to as the "American School," which stood apart from other systems of medicine due to its admonition against mercury and other mineral drugs, opposition to salivation and regimens of depletion, condemnation of bloodletting in all forms, rejection of unnecessary surgery, and choosing from a materia medica that consisted largely of indigenous plant remedies. Although the eclectics flourished through the mid- and late-nineteenth century when the art and science of medicine was undergoing a profound crisis of faith, they are seldom remembered today even though they numbered close to ten thousand by the end of the century. Over the course of their history, some sixty-five schools espoused their beliefs and were accompanied by one national and thirty state societies, and approximately 130 medical journals.

The oldest of the eclectic schools, the Eclectic Medical College of Cincinnati, known affectionately by students, faculty, and alumni as "Old EMI," was a proprietary college representing a consolidation of the Worthington Medical College (1830-42), the American Medical College (1853), the Eclectic College of Medicine and Surgery (1857-59), and the Eclectic Medical Institute (1845-1910). The school changed its name to the Eclectic Medical College in 1910 when it reorganized as a not-for-profit educational institution. During its halcyon days, the school was considered the "Mecca" of eclectic medicine as generations of graduates, including many women, held positions in private practices, colleges, hospitals, insurance companies, governmental sanitary boards, and as surgeons in the army and navy. Many served rural America with dedication and while some became prominent surgeons, these were the exception rather than the rule. In the main, the eclectics were generalists whose availability made them loved and appreciated by their patients. By 1911, the school boasted more than four thousand graduates of which 1,800 were still engaged in practice.

But change was coming to medical education as sectarianism no longer retained the credibility it once held among the general population. As state medical boards raised their entrance requirements beyond the basic high school standard, and as all medical colleges struggled to find the capital to modernize with new laboratories, better equipment, larger hospital facilities, and full-time salaried instructors, many fell by the wayside. Between 1906 and 1914, the number of regular medical colleges declined from 130 to 87, with a 35.4 percent decline in the number of graduates. For homeopathic schools, there was a corresponding decline from 22 to ten schools, with 63.3 percent fewer graduates. For the eclectics, the numbers were even more ominous. From a high of 10 schools in 1910 to 4 in 1914, the eclectics showed a decrease of 68.3 percent in the number of graduates.

Unlike the homeopaths whose history was more prominently recorded and who are still active among alternative and complementary healers in postmodernist medicine, the eclectics receded from the scene, struggling without success to meet the rising standards set by the American Medical Association's Council on Medical Education. The combination of stricter licensing laws, higher admission standards, several notorious scandals involving eclectic diploma mills, and the devastating impact of Abraham Flexner's muckraking classic *Medical Education in the United States and Canada,* published in 1910, brought the eclectic schools to their knees. The eclectics found themselves in the backwaters of modern medicine, unable to break away from their botanic bias and ill-equipped to support the implications of germ theory, the financial costs of salaried faculty and staff, and the research implications of laboratory science. In the decade following Flexner's report, all but one of the remaining eclectic schools closed outright or merged with university-based medical colleges. Only the Eclectic Medical College continued its struggle. The *coup de grace* came in 1935 when the Council on Medical Education announced its refusal to continue grading sectarian schools. With that decision, those few sectarian schools that remained chose to close or disavow their sectarian dogmas for a biomedical curriculum with standards consistent with conventional medical schools.

In 1939, the Eclectic Medical College closed its doors and relinquished its charter in 1942 in exchange for allowing the school's graduates to enter the armed forces with commissions and that any restrictions against securing postgraduate work would be removed, including internship opportunities at approved hospitals. It is ironic, however, that in the last several decades of its existence, upwards of half the school's graduates were no longer defenders of the eclectic philosophy, but Jewish students seeking an alternative route into medicine due to quotas set against them by conventional medical schools. Once graduated, they took their medical degrees and "mainstreamed" back into conventional medicine, thereby cutting off ties to their alma mater.

The story you are about to read concerns the life and times of Wallace W. Wheat who matriculated at the Eclectic Medical Institute in 1896, after deciding to dedicate his life to medicine. Graduating in 1899, Wheat practiced general medicine for more than forty-five years in rural Roseville, Indiana. Drawing from historical records, author Laura Z. Clavio has taken an artist's touch to Wheat's life and times, infusing it with local color and bringing the doctor and his patients to life with dialog. She has accomplished what many historians struggle to achieve, namely, making history more "authentic" by capturing the flavor of an age.

John S. Haller, Jr.
Emeritus Professor of History and Medical Humanities
Southern Illinois University Carbondale

Memorial plaque for Roseville, Indiana. Photo by Laura Clavio

This is historical fiction based on many events in the real lives of Wallace W. Wheat and his family, friends, and colleagues, in Roseville, Indiana. Wallace Wheat is the grandson of John Mulliken Wheat, who arrived in Roseville in 1840.

Thirty-four years earlier, in 1803, President Thomas Jefferson granted Indiana Territorial Governor William Henry Harrison the power to negotiate treaties with Native American tribes for the purchase of land tracts in the Indiana Territory. Harrison spent more than a decade signing treaties with indigenous tribes, or using whatever means were necessary, to complete his task. In 1816 "Harrison's Purchase" opened for land sales.

The land that became the southwest corner of Parke County, Indiana, where this story takes place, was obtained in the Treaty of Fort Wayne in 1809. The northeast border of this land was defined by and dubbed the Ten O'clock Line. The Miami tribal leaders, who claimed ownership, were told this was the line where the shadow of a spear would fall at 10 a.m. Harrison knew this fertile plain along the Wabash River would be attractive to settlers. Shawnee chief Tecumseh unsuccessfully disputed the Miami claim to ownership on behalf of the other tribes that inhabited the land. The dispute was finally settled when Harrison attacked and defeated the Native Americans in the Battle of Tippecanoe in 1811.

In an 1817 edition of *Brown's Gazetteer*, surveyor M.D. Buck published a description of the Wabash Valley in the newly organized state of Indiana. He told readers about rich bottom lands in the western central part of the state, north of Fort William Henry Harrison, with a vegetable top soil that ran twenty-two feet deep. In addition to the Wabash River, he described another tributary, a one-hundred foot-wide Rocky River called Sugar Creek with several large forks meandering through the hills and prairies. He described it as a waterway whose beauty exceeded anything he had ever seen. Buck assured settlers that there was abundant wildlife for food and clothing, including black bears, wolves, deer and wild turkey. He told of apple trees that bore fruit every year, good grazing land for animals and outstanding wild ginseng growing in the bottoms.

Well-to-do people from the East Coast began to purchase tracts of land, tempted either by relocating themselves to establish iconic farms, or by the potential to sell tracts for a profit to settlers in years to come. Initially, land sold in parcels of forty acres for a dollar and a quarter an acre.

Captain Andrew Brooks was an Indian agent, trader, and interpreter who had followed the U.S. Army to Fort Harrison, near present-day Terre Haute, Indiana. He made many exploratory trips looking for good locations for commerce. He found a good spot for a mill on Big Raccoon Creek. Raccoon Valley was in the bottom land below the bluffs created by the termination of the glacial soil push from the north. The wide creek meandered through the valley and emptied into the Wabash several miles north of Brooks' choice mill site.

Brooks had an eye for property but empty pockets when it came to financing his project. In early 1819, he made the acquaintance of a young, ambitious pioneer from Wethersfield Meadows, Connecticut, named Chauncey Rose. Rose had come to Fort Harrison with some money his wealthy merchant brother had advanced to him to establish a business. He and the captain became immediate friends.

Rose was excited about the idea of a good mill on a tributary so close to the Wabash River. Along with a third partner, Moses Robbins, the three men broke ground for the new mill in late winter. Captain Brooks used his negotiating skills and his relationship with the local tribal leaders to help smooth the way for their enterprise. They named the village founded at the location of the mill Roseville because Mr. Rose had provided the financing for the venture.

The firm of Rose, Robbins, and Brooks built the grist mill on the southern bend of the creek where there was a high bank. A rock bed in the creek provided support to build a dam that channeled water for turning the big mill wheel. They also opened a saw mill, a general store and a distillery. The native tribes trusted Brooks and came to trust

Robbins, who they nicknamed "Old Mohawk". They traded heavily with the firm, bringing in furs and meat in exchange for flour, coffee, tobacco and corn whiskey.

The village of Roseville became an important trading post. Another area pioneer named Judge Wedding also opened a store. Robbins and Wedding soon entered into the pork packing business, slaughtering the abundant razor back hogs in the area. Flat boats could be pulled upstream by roping them to trees along the creek and pushing them with long sticks. Then, loaded with barrels full of pork, whiskey and flour, the boats were sent back downstream where they entered the Wabash River for a ride down to New Orleans. When they reached their destination the goods were sold; the boats were dismantled and the hardwood lumber was sold.

Roseville was both a trading post and a stagecoach stop. In 1821, it was named the first county seat of newly drawn Parke County. That didn't last long. The county seat moved to Armiesburg, then to Rockville in 1822. Roseville was a hub for area commerce, though, and played an important role in the economy until about 1835. It was a place full of rough people attracting many itinerant souls - drifters, migrants and the type of women who followed them. Robbins' corn liquor helped ignite many brawls that Brooks, who had been appointed sheriff, had to handle.

Some also came to establish farms and raise their families in this place still so rich with the gifts of nature. A man could find everything he needed to build a home on his own property. The creek supplied bountiful water and fish. Old growth trees provided plenty of timber for building a home and a barn. The farmers grew crops of wheat, corn, oats and clover seed. They established orchards, and they raised cattle, chickens, ducks, geese and pigs.

The Wheat Family Comes To Roseville

John Mulliken Wheat moved his young family from Washington, D.C. to Richmond, Indiana, in 1837. He was an enterprising young farmer looking for good land. He traveled to western Indiana to see the land and recommended an investment there to his father, John Wheat, Jr. His father, a former plantation owner whose land had become part of the newly created United States capital of Washington, D.C., purchased 160 acres of land in Florida Township, Parke County.

John Mulliken Wheat moved with his family to Roseville in 1840 to establish the new farm. His wife Miriam was a feisty woman of Irish descent who grew up in Baltimore, Maryland. She had been less excited about the move, but she went where her husband took her. The couple had three children: Caroline, Benjamin, and Edward Leander, who was nicknamed Lee.

Life in western Indiana was a far cry from the bustling city life of Baltimore. Miriam died of a fever later that year. A slave couple that John Mulliken had brought with them from Washington, D.C., but who were freed upon their arrival in Parke County, remained with John to help on the farm and raise the children.

John Mulliken Wheat inherited the Florida Township land when his father died in 1843, and left the land to his children when he died in 1851.

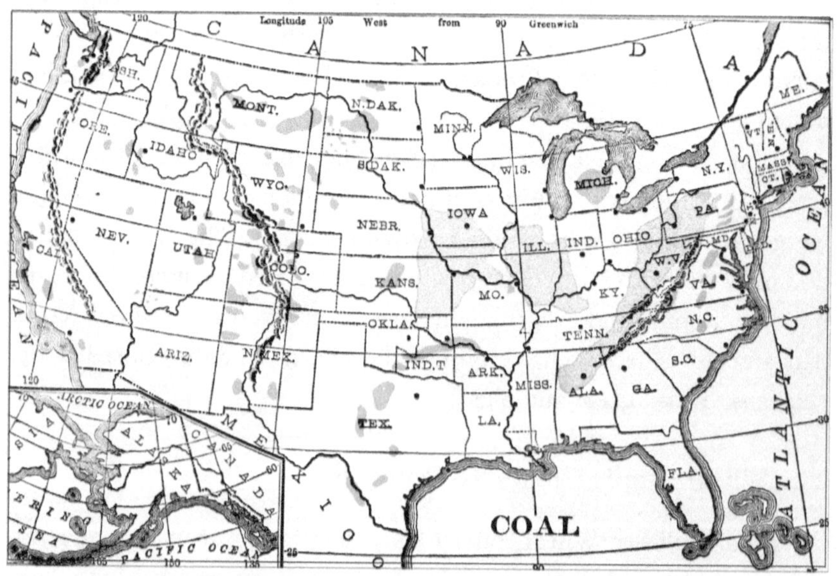

Coal Map. Advanced Geography by Alexis Everett Frye, published in 1900

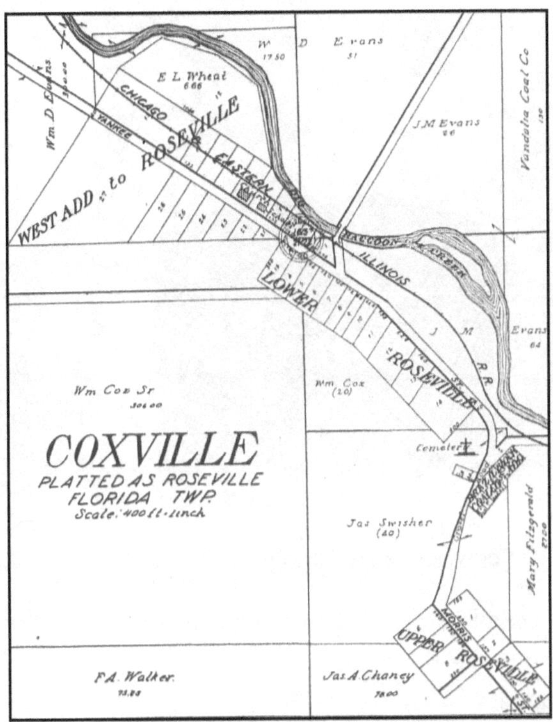

Early plat map with E. L. Wheat property. Courtesy of Parke County Historical Society

How Roseville Came To Have Two Names

After the Civil War coal came to prominence in the Midwest as fuel for the forging fires of blacksmiths and to heat homes. In 1872, Joseph Martin from nearby Brazil, Indiana, opened the first Parke County coal mine. Another settlement up the hill to the west of Roseville sprang up with new people moving in to work the mines. It was named Coxville after Mr. William Cox, who owned most of the land and nearly all the mining rights in the area.

To serve the growing number of mines in the area, the Momence and Brazil Railroad put a line of track parallel to Big Raccoon Creek through Roseville. When the Brazil Block Coal Company bought some coal mining rights in the area, the company renamed the town after Mr. Cox. The railroad went along with the change and named the

The Roseville Covered Bridge 2011. Photo by Laura Clavio

station the Coxville Stop. When the town was granted a post office, it was done so under the name of Coxville, much to the chagrin of the Roseville residents.

A petition was sent to the Parke County courts to restore the name of Roseville, and the name was eventually restored. Ever since, there has been great confusion over the proper name of the town. Most now just refer to it as Coxville/Roseville.

The Roseville Covered Bridge

Today, Parke County calls itself "The Covered Bridge Capital of the World" with 31 covered bridges still standing. The Roseville covered bridge was built by J. J. Daniels who had constructed many bridges in western Indiana. Its three-hundred-feet span over Big Raccoon Creek was a vital connection for the village with the coal mines and farmland they worked located on the high ridge. While the bridge covers were built to protect the wooden beams from rotting, they also made the bridges picturesque. The bridges offered refuge for travelers in the rain, relief from the beating sun in summer and shelter from the relentless wind of a winter storm.

ONE

"Look out below!"

Doctor Wheat yelled to his nieces and nephews from atop a ladder he had positioned against the greenhouse roof. He was about to knock off the icicles that had formed along the roof's edge, and he didn't want to hit anyone as he whacked the icicles with a broom handle. They broke off with a high-pitched ping and landed like daggers in the snow below with a muffled thud.

It was late afternoon of November 20, 1929. A massive and slow-moving snowstorm had deposited over a foot of snow in Big Raccoon Valley. Such a load on a glass house might be more than the structure could bear. Doc had recruited as much help as he could to relieve pressure on the building. A half dozen people now worked to shake snow off the canvas covering of the roof with whatever brooms or poles they could find to reach its peak.

Reaching out so far stretched his aging muscles. The cold air challenged his breathing. Just standing on the ladder was more painful than he imagined, and he stifled a groan, not wanting the children to hear him complain. He was so intent on controlling his pain and on completing his task that, at first, he didn't hear his name being called.

"Doc. Doc!" A familiar voice that seemed to shout with a sense of urgency reached him. He looked down to see young Russell Cottrell trudging toward him through the yard. The son of Paul "Babe" Cottrell, a friend and business colleague, Doc was amazed to see him.

Doc called to him, "Up here! Russell, what are you doing here? How did you get here?"

"I walked. I guess I ran most of the way," Russell replied. "Doc, you gotta come now. Ma's in labor!" he said trying to catch his breath. He had walked as fast as he could manage through the snow, covering nearly five miles from his home on Tick Ridge to the doctor's office only to find that he was not there. He had trudged the extra quarter mile to the house hoping the doctor would be there. His lungs were nearly frozen, his feet and hands numb. The young man looked up at Doc through the falling snow. Doc was bundled up in his warm plaid woolen coat, scarf, a hunting cap with the ear flaps pulled down, a pair of wool pants and knee high boots. He looked more like a lumberjack than a doctor in that getup, but he didn't care. It kept him warm. Doc leaned on the ladder for a minute as he looked down.

"You sure about that, Russell? Bit early, isn't it?" Doc asked. "She's only about eight months along."

"Yes, sir, I know. But Pa says it's happening, and you need to come right away."

Russell was anxious, and Doc knew that Babe wouldn't have sent for him without cause. From his high perch, Doc looked out over the flood plain and to the road that led to Tick Ridge. The ground was piled high with snow. The wind was picking up, blowing great swirls of snowflakes into the air where they sparkled and danced on the breeze.

"Well, I guess we better get a move on. I think Charlie is in the house. Go tell him to get the car," he told Russell. "Then warm yourself up by the fire, son. Have Nellie fix you some hot chocolate. It's good for you."

"Yes, sir."

Doc had purchased a new Model A Ford earlier in the year. He didn't drive cars. Never had. Never would. He felt uncomfortable and out of control behind the wheel of a car, so he decided years ago that he would not drive. He depended on others to get him where he needed to go. He had decided that he would concentrate on being the doctor. They could concentrate on being drivers. He still preferred his horse and buggy when the house call was close enough. But, the world had become an impatient place. Buggies on the road were in constant danger from impudent drivers who honked their horns and scared the horses. For the sake of the animals and his own peace of mind he had given in to a mechanized mode of transportation. He was glad he had good friends and family members who were willing to assist in getting him to his patients.

He slowly descended the ladder while Russell held it for him. It wasn't easy for him. It was painful for his feet to step on the ladder rungs. He shook the excess snow from his coat. Russell headed for the house and found Charlie.

Charlie Brown, who tended the horses and machinery for Doc's farm, often drove Doc on house calls. He went to the barn to get the car. It was a high-wheel model with a chassis high off the ground. It could handle driving through the mounting snow. The car was only a two-seater, a small model that was just big enough to meet the doctor's needs. There was no room for Russell, so he would have to walk back home. Charlie pulled up in front of the house. Doc climbed in, and they headed back to his office. Doc went in to grab his instruments and his medical bag. They drove through the covered bridge; then, down into the flood plain they rode to the base of the hills. It was then a slow, treacherous drive up ice-covered Fisher Road to the top of the ridge.

The Cottrell family lived in a two-room cabin where they had moved after the store Babe owned in Coxville had burned to the ground. The fire started when a customer carelessly left his burning cigar on a shelf. Babe smelled smoke in the middle of the night and found the lower level of the store engulfed in flames. The family barely escaped from their quarters above the store. Babe and his wife Hallie had strapped their four children inside of their bed mats and tossed them out the window to safety. The couple had to jump from the second story. The family lost everything and had to move to the cabin owned by Babe's mother. Now Babe worked farming Doc's land for a living.

Hallie was giving birth to their seventh child, although only four of the children had survived. Doc had been there for them all. Paul, the eldest son, and his father were awaiting Doc's arrival. His sisters, Ruby and Wilma, were tending to their mother. Doc noticed a litter of three baby pigs that had been born just a few days ago were being kept warm in a small box on the open door of the cook stove. As darkness fell, the outside temperature plummeted, and the room grew cold just a few feet from the stove.

Doc had Paul hang a blanket on a piece of rope in front of Hallie's bed while he examined his patient. Her labor pains were coming about five minutes apart, so he knew they were in time and, in fact, had some time to wait. He looked through the medical items he had brought, only to cluck in disgust.

"Charlie, I should have been more careful. I walked off without my forceps. Do you know what I'm talking about?" Doc held out his hands moving them in and out gesturing the way one might when operating bellows. He wanted Charlie to understand the tong-like medical instrument he was looking for.

"I'm afraid I'm going to have to send you back to the office to get it. I can't afford not to have them if things don't go right, you understand? I don't like this, don't like it at all. But I want to be prepared for anything."

Charlie nodded. "Ok, Doc. I know what you are talking about." He had accompanied Doc on many births and the medical instruments were not a mystery to him.

"I must have put them in the instrument drawer in the medicine chest," Doc guessed. "Get back as soon as you can!"

"OK, Doc." Charlie started for the door. He hadn't yet thawed out from the trip, but he didn't waste time worrying about it. He set off back down the treacherous road in the snow-covered car.

Doc worked with Hallie. He felt her stomach. The baby seemed to be in good position, and he knew that Hallie had normal deliveries before. He wasn't terribly worried, except for the probable condition of the baby, which he knew was going to be very small.

He pushed the hanging blanket aside to help better distribute the heat in the room and began to examine the room for ideas on how to keep the baby warm and alive when it came. He sent Paul out to fetch more water from the well. He filled a pot with water from a bucket and put it on the stove. Hallie was strong and complained little. An almost full blooded Cherokee she rarely spoke to anyone and kept both her pain and her emotions to herself. Doc looked at her with admiration. He had been delivering babies for thirty years. By now he could predict with fair accuracy the women who would come through childbirth with little trauma and those who would suffer from the experience.

Doc had put on some of weight of late, and his cheeks were fleshy and full. It was unusual for him, because he had been fit and active his whole life. At age 59, he still had a full head of graying sandy brown hair. It was just slightly curly and he wore it parted on the left and swept back from his face. He often touched up the gray with some henna coloring. He had a broad forehead and a ready smile. His eyes were bright ice blue and gleamed with intensity and purpose. He hadn't been as active of late. It was more difficult to move around now, and he just didn't have the same stamina anymore. He tried not to let others know about how much pain he dealt with daily. He did not medicate himself for pain. He figured he had pain for a reason and it wasn't helping the body to cover it up.

Doctor Wheat had returned to Roseville many years ago. It was a homecoming that marked the culmination of his journey from the small boy who wandered the nearby hills and swept out his father's pharmacy and general store to the competent physician who served this rural village. He could have made a lot more money practicing in Indianapolis, living like a king, but he came back here. Folks thought he was either extremely loyal to his family and friends or just a plain fool. Whatever his reason for returning, his patients and his neighbors had grown dependent upon him. Patients from many places far from Parke County had sought out "the herb doctor of the Wabash Valley" as he had come to be called over the years.

An hour passed, and Doc Wheat became lost in thought as he stared at the fire in the stove. Hallie moaned softly. Babe sat beside her holding her hand. Doc examined her once again and listened to her heart. He listened to the faint, rapid beat of the baby's heart. Contractions were about a minute apart now. He gave her a cloth to bite down on. It wouldn't be much longer, but Charlie still hadn't returned with the forceps. Doc was concerned that he wouldn't make it back in time. He felt the position of the baby once more. It seemed very small but positioned well. Likely, the birth would go smoothly. Still, Doc would have felt more comfortable if he had all the needed tools at hand. He admonished himself for walking off without such a critical instrument. He never used to do things like that!

Doc had no idea how many babies he had delivered, and he really had no desire to keep a count. He had seen more times than he cared to recall the pain and the agony of delivery and the sometimes devastating consequences of childbirth. Delivering babies had become a bigger part of his practice than he had ever imagined. It had been fascinating to watch all those babies grow into vibrant young people. As the years passed he enjoyed talking with of all those youngsters he had helped bring into the world, and they always delighted in a visit with the doctor.

Doc had also developed a great respect for women. He knew how important good care was to help the mothers survive and be there to raise their children. Even though there was a modern hospital nearby in Clinton, most folks couldn't afford to spend money on a hospital just to have a baby. The country doctor was still the one who attended births.

Hallie was ready to push when a snow-covered Charlie returned with both Doc's missing instrument and Russell.

"Sorry, Doc! I got stuck in a snow drift at the bottom of the hill," Charlie related in his apology. "It's a good thing Russell came along about then. He helped dig me out!"

Doc gave Russell a congratulatory pat on the shoulder, then he quickly took the forceps plopping it into the boiling water on the stove. He ordered Babe to pull the blanket across between the bed and where the children sat in the kitchen so that they would not have to watch the birth.

When the crown of the baby's head began to emerge Doc encouraged Hallie to push. That was all it took for the tiny baby to appear. Doc held the baby in the palm of his hand. She could not weigh more than three pounds. A small slap on her bottom and the baby began to cry.

"Hallie, you have a daughter!" Doc exclaimed. "I guess the women now have the advantage in this household," he added with a laugh. Hallie smiled at him as the built-up muscular tension of childbirth eased and she began to relax.

Doc set the child down on her stomach while he tied and cut the birth cord. He then carried the baby over to a table where he gently washed her with some warm water from the stove. He rubbed the baby girl all over with olive oil and wrapped her in a little blanket. He cradled her in his arm to share his body warmth with her as he checked to make sure her nasal passages and mouth were clear. Her cries were tiny and shrill, but her lungs seemed to be functioning well.

Babe watched it all as he held his wife's hand. He needed the warmth of contact with her, and he gently kissed the back of her hand. He was a short, thin man with dark coloring and dark brown eyes. Ruby cleaned Hallie's face with a soft cloth. Babe smiled at his wife, but didn't speak. There was no need. Their feelings for one another were communicated with just a loving look after so many years together.

The cold winter night left no option as to where the child must be kept. She would never survive away from the warmth of the stove, not even in her mother's arms. Doc explained the situation to Babe. He then told his children that the baby pigs would have to take their chances further from the stove if their sister was going to live. The pigs were moved to make room for the baby. Little Doris Rose, as she was to be called by her parents, was placed in a shoebox on the stove door.

"Doris Rose, you have been given the place of honor!" Doc told the tiny girl as he gently laid her on a comfy blanket in the box. "The world has welcomed you with a genuine blizzard, but you have been invited into a good family!"

Wilma had huddled in the corner of the room watching all the activity. She walked over to the stove and looked at the baby in the box. Her eyes were large and questioning as she pulled back the corner of the cloth to get a closer look. The baby, seeming to sense someone near, raised startled arms in the air. Wilma reached for the little hand and held it between her fingers. She looked up at Doc.

"She's so tiny, so helpless."

Doc looked at the girl. He came over and leaned down on one knee looking into the box with her. He took the baby's other hand, his thumb larger than her whole hand.

"Yes, she is. It is hard to believe that you and I started out this way, too. That's why we need mothers and fathers, brothers and sisters to help us and take care of us while we grow up. You will help, won't you?

Wilma looked at him and nodded with a big grin.

Doc then turned his attention to Hallie to check her for tears along the birth canal and to wait for the afterbirth. After she was finished and cleaned up he went to his medical bag where, secured along its inside, were rows of small bottles marked "Specific Medicine". Into one small bottle which held a bit of wine he mixed Black Cohosh root and Black Haw bark extracts which would help with after pains. Into another bottle he put Blue Cohosh root extract which would help prevent postpartum hemorrhage. He left instructions for Babe on how to administer the dosage and how often Hallie would need to take the medicine.

Babe made some cornmeal mush for them all and then the children settled down on the floor to sleep. Babe stayed with his wife the rest of the night. Doc kept a close eye on the newborn. She was breathing remarkably well for one so small. Her color was good, and she gave out a cry that Doc interpreted as hunger. He took the baby to Hallie, who put the child to her breast where Doris Rose sucked her first meal. Babe lay on the other side of the child to give additional warmth while she fed. She was then returned to the box on the stove.

By first light the snow had finally stopped falling. The sunlight reflected on the glimmering crystal-white coating on the hillsides, still unspoiled by the heat of day. The child had survived the night. Unfortunately, the baby pigs had not. Charlie pulled the car out of the barn and started it. He and the doctor rode slowly down the icy roadway toward home.

Doc had been able to catch only a few winks of sleep throughout the night. It wasn't his habit to sleep much, but, today, he felt tired. As he rode along the ridge he could see the remnants of the old grist mill upstream from the bridge. Roseville had not been an important town now for nearly a hundred years, but coal mining had kept the village moving forward through the early 1900s. Now, it was just a quiet, out-of-the–way place to live.

Doc looked at the brightly painted covered bridge. Except for time when he was away at school, he had never lived more than ten miles from that bridge. He and that bridge shared history together. His mind floated back to past days with his family as Charlie steered the car, picking its way along the rutted and snow-covered road.

TWO

"It's your move, Lee."

The deep, yet gentle and controlled voice that prodded belonged to Pastor Ward. He sat opposite his friend across a checkerboard that was balanced on top of a wooden crate. In 1870, June fifth was hot and humid. The moisture clung to all like an unwanted blanket. Lee Wheat and Pastor Jonathan Ward had shed their coats as they sat under a shade tree near Lee's house filled with activity that the men neither cared to share nor were welcome to participate in as two women tended to his wife who was giving birth.

Lee eyed his friendly adversary looking for clues to his tactics. Neither man was quick to make a move and cautiously contemplated things far beyond the board before placing a hand on the checker to advance the game. The anxiety that childbirth brought along with the potential for grief that had resulted on several occasions was almost more than Lee could bear. Losing himself in checkers was a humane and acceptable escape.

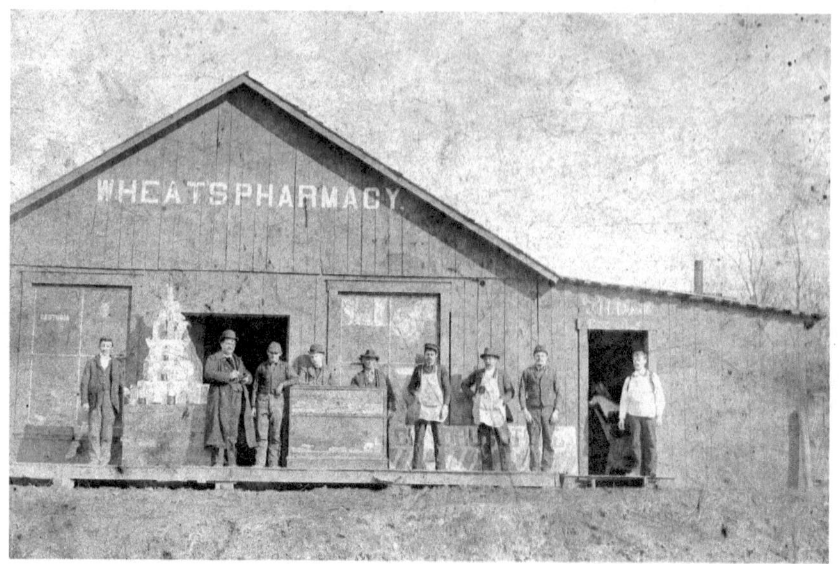

Wheat Pharmacy in Roseville circa 1875. Courtesy of Galloway Photo

Lee operated the family farm and also ran a general store and pharmacy that he opened in Roseville in the late 1850s. His brother Ben chose a military career and came home only sporadically until the end of the War Between the States. Even though he worked on the farm through his late teen years, Ben never had any real interest in being a farmer.

Lee fell in love with Margaret Ann Nail, a woman of Pennsylvania German descent from Shelbyville, Indiana. Nine years younger than he, her gentle countenance, enhanced by her sweet smile, beautiful auburn hair and bright blue eyes captured his heart. They married in Roseville's neighboring village of Mecca in 1859. When the South withdrew from the Union and war was declared, Lee found that his profession as a merchant exempted him from military service.

The couple lost their first two children. Albert was born strong and robust in 1863, and Frank came along two years later. Then, twins born in 1866 lived but three weeks. Horace was born two years later.

Lee's sister, Caroline, had married Harmon Hagar in 1846. A daughter, Lizzie, was born to them ten years later. Harmon was

Margaret Ann Wheat with infant, Albert Wheat.
Courtesy of Galloway Photo

conscripted to fight for the Union in 1863. He left not knowing he had a second child on the way. Edward Hagar was born in 1864. Harmon Hagar never returned from the war, and no word of him was ever received.

When Caroline, weakened by grief and struggle, died in 1869, Lee and Margaret Ann took guardianship of Lizzie and Edward. After

Caroline's death, Lee put a portion of the farm up for sale. With his share of the money he purchased a six-acre tract of land in Roseville and built a two-story home near his store on Yankee Street. He retained three tracts of prime farmland, two in the bottom land and one tract on top of the ridge past the Vandalia Coal Mine.

Pastor Ward ministered for a newly formed Methodist Episcopal church that had split off from the town's established parish. His growing congregation met in a two-story house just a little farther down on Yankee Street. The house also served as the school building. He had come to sit with his good friend and share his anxious moments.

Annalee Marshall, a midwife, well-known for her skills in bringing women through childbirth, cared for Margaret Ann. A neighbor, Mrs. Bynum, kept a pot of fresh water boiling on the fire the men built in the yard where she had earlier boiled linens for the baby. With two glasses of lemonade in hand, she walked over to where the men were playing checkers and offered the refreshment. They gratefully accepted.

"Mr. Wheat, I do believe that you are trying to fill the church all by yourself!" she said with a laugh as she commented on the growing size of his family.

"Mrs. Bynum, there is plenty of room in that church. I'm only happy to be making my contributions." Mr. Wheat laughed gently at her comments.

"You know, this will be the seventh birth, Mr. Wheat. Oh, I know that they ain't all lived, but, the seventh child, if it is the seventh boy child; well he's likely to be a special one. The seventh child is likely to be a healer. That's what they say," Mrs. Bynum predicted.

Lee and Pastor Ward looked inquisitively at one another and then at Mrs. Bynum. It was not the first time that she had made predictions, and she had demonstrated an uncanny knack for knowing the future. Her ability to "know" things was a bit unsettling to most folks around. She was careful to offer only positive notions.

"Well, Mrs. Bynum, I hope you're right," Lee said cautiously. "I do hope you're right. We could certainly use a doctor around here. Yes, indeed. If this child turns out to be a doctor, I would be most proud."

"It will be a boy, Mr. Wheat," Mrs. Bynum promised. "You'll see. I'm not wrong on this."

"Another boy? Mrs. Bynum, you have all my best thoughts that your predictions are accurate," Lee responded as he stroked his dark mustache. He was a short, stout man with graying dark hair. A generous smile lit his round face.

The children had been ordered outside and given chores to keep them occupied and out of the way. Lizzie was fourteen and helped her brother Edward peel potatoes for dinner. They kept a close eye on two-year-old Horace playing on the ground beside them.

Albert, who would soon be seven, and five-year-old Frank came back from the woods across the road where they gathered firewood. They dropped their load at the woodpile near the house and started to run for the front door. Their father's command halted them.

"Now boys, stay out of the house 'til this birthin' is over," Lee called to them. Frank ran over to see the checker game.

"Father, will Mommy have a puppy?" Frank asked. "I want one." Lee and Pastor Ward laughed loudly.

"No, Frank," said his father. "And, we have enough mouths to feed around here without a puppy! You're going to have to settle for a baby brother or sister. Or, you can go down to the barn and look after a cat or one of those baby pigs."

"We'll all know soon if it is a boy or girl, Frank. Just wait a little longer," Pastor Ward assured him.

The men heard screaming from inside the house. No matter how unnerving it seemed they remained frozen with eyes fixed on the checkerboard. Soon the screams were followed by the sound of tiny cries. Lizzie dropped her paring knife and ran to the door to peek in. A bit later, Mrs. Bynum came out of the house.

"Well, Mr. Wheat, you are a father once again. You have a fine looking son."

"Well, well! That's good news! Fine news, Mrs. Bynum," Lee responded as he gave her a quick hug. He wiped his forehead with a handkerchief as the tension dropped from his face with word that his wife and child were well.

"Congratulations, Lee!" Pastor Ward said as he vigorously shook Lee's hand and slapped him on the back.

"What do you plan on calling the boy?" Mrs. Bynum asked. Lee pondered the question momentarily.

"Well, I told Mrs. Wheat that she should name this child. I've named most of the others. Mrs. Wheat said that if it was a boy we should call him Wallace W."

"Wallace W. Wheat. Three W's. That should be a powerful name for a strong man, Mr. Wheat," said Mrs. Bynum. "Three of anything is always a lucky number!"

Albert and Frank ran up and hugged their father. He embraced them hard releasing some of the pent up emotion that he had held back all day. Annalee stepped through the doorway onto the porch.

"Mr. Wheat, you can come and see your wife and new son now," she said smiling proudly.

Lee glanced quickly at his children and patted each boy on the head. He nodded to Pastor Ward and walked swiftly toward the door. He crossed the threshold and with just three steps stood in the doorway of the bedroom where his wife lay weak from the effort. The baby was tightly wrapped in a swaddling cloth and tucked in neatly beside her. Lee crossed the room and knelt at her side stroking back her tangled hair and searching her eyes as if to reassure himself that love for him still resided there. He looked down at the child and stroked his forehead then looked back at his wife.

"Congratulations, Lee," she whispered. "You have another son!"

THREE

"Out of my kitchen, both of you!" Margaret Ann sent two of her brood of young boys out the back door with buckets. "Fill those buckets three times, do you hear?"

Happy years passed as the Wheat family continued to grow.

Wallace and his brother Horace trudged down to the creek bank to fulfill their chore. They were constant companions causing boyish mischief of many kinds, and they were constantly shooed away from the house by their mother who found them underfoot too often. The boys occasionally earned a swat on the behind with a broom and were frequently dispatched with buckets to the creek for water as punishment. Little brothers Scott, Dayton and Lee, Jr. would often tag along.

Margaret Ann was a small woman, but she did not let her size undermine her command of the family. She kept herself neat and presentable at all times and wore her hair parted in the center, tied back into a compact bun at the base of her neck. She did not possess superior beauty, but she had a kind, generous nature that radiated from her very presence. It didn't take much to bring a smile to her face or to make her laugh, but her gritty, no nonsense side would take over when she was pushed too far. She was tough minded for one so young. She had to be with so many youngsters to manage. Yet she offered a warm embrace to the boys when they needed it, and they adored her.

She enjoyed reading and allowed herself some time to do so in the quiet hours after the children were in bed as she sipped a cup of blackberry leaf tea. Her home was filled with love and her kitchen with good food. There was always potpourri simmering on the stove to scent the air inside the house with the sweet smell of flowers and herbs. There were sachets of lemon balm and mint in the dresser drawers to freshen the clothing and discourage crawling visitors. The heady aroma of cedar filled the wardrobe to discourage moths, fleas and mosquitoes. She kept her home clean and scrubbed and welcomed family and friends to visit. She generously shared her life with those around her and did many things for the community.

Wallace looked like his mother with a fair complexion and a shank of sandy red hair. His blue eyes seemed to sparkle from beneath low-sloping eyelids whenever an interesting thought ignited his brain. He had a happy, engaging disposition. A precocious six-year-old, his intelligence was evident. His sharp wit sometimes led to trouble when he would correct an elder. He was skinny, but strong and energetic.

His eldest brother, Albert, already had his adult growth. He was short, standing only five feet, eight inches, and solidly built with a square face, light brown hair and blue eyes. He was a plain young man with a broad forehead reminiscent of his father and his Uncle Ben. He was the designated leader of the siblings and charged with keeping his many brothers in line. Brother Frank had his father's dark hair and eyes and a quiet nature that tended to make him less noticed than his brothers. He was happiest when tending to the farm animals, and he had a special love for the horses.

Horace had the same stout build and coloring as Albert. He didn't care for school. He was in constant motion and very difficult to contain. He was easily distracted and hated having to sit in a schoolhouse. For him, the best learning was "out there", not in a book. He could not concentrate on his lessons. It was everything he could to do stay in his seat. He was the first one out the door after school headed toward the woods for a good run.

Wallace was closest in age to Horace and had just started school. He followed Horace everywhere. He found excitement in his brother's pranks, but he had a more serious nature. They caught toads to frighten girls and dug worms for fishing in Big Raccoon Creek. The boys caught crawdads under the spans of the covered bridge and carried home many creatures that received no welcome from their mother. Frank taught them how to feed the pigs and chickens, and they did other simple chores as part of their big family. Everyone worked on the crops.

Caroline's son, Edward Hager, moved out to take work in Terre Haute. His sister Lizzie had married and lived nearby. She and another young wife often took the four youngest Wheat boys to gather seeds, berries, herbs and greens. A few juicy berries from the bucket were given as a little reward. In late summer and fall they would gather the harvest of wild food—persimmons, apples, wild cherries and plums. Walnuts were abundant and served as a cash crop as well. Foraged food was divided among the families.

Margaret Ann took great pleasure in Wallace to the point where the other boys thought he might be her favorite. Who knew if it was true? Life was too busy to contemplate such trivial things, and jealousy was an emotion that was not welcome or tolerated. Wallace seemed to thrive on her attention. Life had been good to the family. Lee was a competent merchant, and the store provided a good income. His new appointment as the first postmaster of Coxville also came with a salary. The farm yielded ample crops most years.

Margaret Ann was once again pregnant in 1876. Eleven pregnancies in sixteen years had taken their toll on her. She was weak and had to take to her bed. Wallace could see that his mother was not feeling well. He spent time by her bedside reading from the simple books he could decipher or telling her fairy tales and made-up stories about the creatures of the woods to her delight. She would stroke his face and speak lovingly to him about the things she valued. He would lie by her side with his hand on her belly and feel the small kicks from the life inside her womb.

On March 17, 1877, Margaret Ann gave birth to a daughter, but the child died almost immediately. Margaret hemorrhaged, and the loss of blood was quickly becoming critical. Dr. Robert Baldridge, the new village doctor, was called. He tried several doses of tincture of Ergot made from Rye Ergot, but it was inadequate to stop the bleeding.

"There is nothing else to be done," he told Lee Wheat. "It's just a matter of time before she goes."

Lee was devastated by the news that she would not recover. He struggled with how he would tell the children. The next day friends began to gather in the Wheat home, and the Wheat children were brought into the bedroom one by one to say good-bye to their mother.

Wallace was frightened when he took his father's hand and entered the darkened room lit only by two small candles in the corner. Margaret Ann looked up and called him over. Wallace jumped onto the bed and threw his arms around his mother. He noticed that her big tummy was gone. They stayed bound together for several minutes until Margaret Ann spoke to him.

"Wallace, look at me. Look at me." Wallace sat back and obeyed her request, as she struggled to speak.

"You are so very special to me, dear. You must make me a promise," she said in a voice that was barely audible, "that you will mind your father, that you will look after your brothers, and that you will serve your family and the people you know. Do you think you can do that for your mother?"

Wallace's eyes filled with tears. He nodded.

"But, Mommy, you'll be here, won't you? I'll be good, I promise. I'll do anything you ask. Just tell me! Only don't leave. Don't leave," he sobbed and grabbed her once again with the hardest hug he could muster.

"I wish I could stay, my darling," his mother whispered, "but I think that the Lord has other plans for me. You all must love one another as I love you, do you hear?"

"Yes, Mommy. Mommy, please don't go!" he cried.

"Wallace, come," he heard his father say behind him.

"No! I want to stay with Mommy!" Wallace sobbed.

"Please, son. Come with me," his father said gently as he coaxed him away from his mother's side. Wallace slowly let go of his mother's hand as his father half walked him, half pulled him toward the door. He looked at his mother for as long as he was allowed.

"Mommy!" His eyes burned and his heart felt as if it were going to explode as he sobbed uncontrollably. As his brother Scott was taken into his mother's bedroom Wallace ran out the door, across the road and into the woods, the only place he knew to go for solace.

Margaret Ann died later in the day. The family was devastated. The household had seen the very light of their lives snuffed out, and not one handled it well. Lee had seen his mother, his sister, and now his wife taken from him. He was left to face life raising seven boys and with no life partner to help him. He could find no words for his children to ease their sorrow or his own except that the death of their mother was the Lord's will and that she would be in heaven.

Wallace felt that a deep hole had been carved into the center of his body, and his mind held only thoughts of grief. How could Mommy have been taken from him? Where was she going? He flopped down on the woodland carpet of leaves and cried. All the creatures seemed to fall silent as they shared his grief. The wind stirred the leaves; the hoot owl hooted low and soft; the mockingbird whispered a sad and haunting call. All did their best to caress the child. Albert found him hours later and took him home.

———————

FOUR

"There. I think that looks nice, don't you?" Mrs. Fisher, whose husband ran another store down the street in Roseville, stood back to look at the wreath of fresh pine branches that she had hung above the fireplace mantle to help the family celebrate Christmas. The house had no decorations, and Mrs. Fisher thought that the smell of fresh pine in the house might lift everyone's spirits.

"Yes, ma'am," responded Wallace and Horace who stood in the room while their guest completed her task. They tried to generate weak smiles so that she would not feel bad about her efforts to comfort them, but all they really wanted was for her to leave.

The Wheat home was a quiet, dismal place to be for months following Margaret Ann's death. The boys were sullen and listless, and Lee found it difficult to effectively deal with the children's grief. His strength was being put to the test. He tried to project a positive attitude around the boys, but it only thinly veiled his feelings.

"Well, now, Mrs. Fisher, that does look lovely!" said Eliza as she walked into the room from the kitchen. "What would you think if I added a touch of red ribbon to it?"

Lee had hired Eliza Armstrong, a relative from the Virginia side of the family, to maintain the house, cook for the family, and look after the children. An unmarried woman, she seemed to be competent help, but he really didn't even notice her most of the time. His heart was empty and his mind was filled with guilt at the thought that he had lost his love because children just kept on coming. At night, it was not unusual to find one of the boys crying in his sleep or calling out for mother. It was a wound that only time would heal. The only way to cope was for everyone to keep busy.

In the right season, Lee took Horace, Wallace and Frank on occasional long treks into the woods to harvest the herbs that he sold at the store. They might cover several miles in a day until they had all they could carry home. They dug roots of may apple, ginseng, goldenseal and bloodroot in the fall. Some were sold fresh. Others were scrubbed and set out to dry on racks in the barn or shed to be sold to pharmaceutical manufacturers. Berries and bark were dried the same way.

In spring and early summer, leaves of nettles, mint, boneset, comfrey, lemon balm and many other plants were hung upside down on their stems until dried, then, the leaves were stripped from the stems and stored in jars or bags. Even with all this work, what they produced was a small percentage of the preparations carried in the pharmacy. Aside from these and other packaged herbs, the store carried patent medicines, laxatives and teas that local women would use in homemade medicinal preparations. They serviced the few doctors who lived in the area.

Eliza had turned out to be a pretty good cook, and the boys began to accept her into their lives. She always had a smile for them. She would tuck special little treats like a fig or a hard candy into the lunch bags that they took to school or out to the fields. Her cheerfulness lightened the sullen mood of the household. She seemed to know what made boys tick, and she was unflappable at the sight of bugs, frogs and worms that they would bring home to see if they could get a reaction from her.

It was nearly a year after the death of their mother that life began to find a new normal. The boys grew closer to one another. Everyone helped in the fields. Everyone had some responsibility at the store. The older boys helped the younger ones with their school-work.

"Wallace, it's your day go clean the outhouse. Will you get to it?" Albert commanded.

"Yes, sir!" Wallace saluted and began to refer to his older brother Albert as "Colonel", as he acted somewhat as a second father to his younger brothers.

Albert carried much of the responsibility for day to day operation of the business. While called a pharmacy, it was really a general store, and it carried most of the everyday items people needed in their small community—groceries, farm supplies, mining gear and clothing. The brothers spent their idle time mastering the game of checkers, playing atop a barrel on the long front porch of the store with the men who dropped by to visit or get a haircut at the barber shop.

Through the years, Wheat's Pharmacy was always a gathering place for the men of the village. The local papers were posted on a bulletin board on the front of the store for passers-by to read. Posters of upcoming events were displayed on the other side of the storefront's large double door, which was left open when weather permitted to let light and air into the interior of the nearly windowless building.

The train made daily stops in Coxville—mornings heading north and evenings south. Henry Crawford had opened a quarry just to the east of Roseville, the source of a very high quality grade of glass sand. The railroad, now owned by the C & EI railroad, had built a switch line back to the quarry, and the loaded cars would be added to the passing train.

The boys especially enjoyed trips to the maple woods in late winter. In the northern part of the county, the woods were thick with old growth sugar maple trees. The sap would run for a couple of weeks each year when the temperature rose to the low forties. In the sugar camps, cooking shacks held big vats of sap to process into syrup. It was a sweet adventure in late February or early March to help with the gathering of the sap buckets.

Acres of maple trees would be tapped by pounding a spout into the side of the tree. Buckets were hung on the taps to catch the sap. Each tree yielded gallons of sap that had to be loaded onto horse-drawn wagons and taken to the sugar house where it would be boiled down over log fires. It took 45 gallons of sap to make one gallon of syrup. Warm drinks and simple snacks would be available for the workers. Sap gathering was even older than the settlements of the early 1800s. The Miami and other native tribes had taught the early settlers about the trees and their bounty.

As spring's blossoms began to appear on the trees in April, it was once again time to turn attention to gathering herbs and medicinal plants. Plants yielded different medicinal properties before and after flowering. It was important to know just when a plant part was ready for harvest. Often there was only a short window of time to catch a plant at its peak. The work was intense throughout May and June when many herbs rapidly reached maturity.

Proper identification of each plant was crucial. Many had poisonous look-alikes. It was especially important during the season when tasty morel mushrooms and other fungi sprouted under the canvas of big trees. Poisonous look-alikes could mean painful abdominal cramps or even death. Spring rains always slowed the herb gathering process. Two or three days of dry weather would need to pass before gathering could begin again, or mold caused by too much moisture on the plant material would spoil the harvest.

In summer, a highlight for the family was a trip to the circus that would come to Rockville once a year. There was a parade down Ohio Street with colorful wagons carrying exotic animals, usually lions and tigers. Women dressed in revealing costumes rode prancing horses and camels. The boys were amazed to see elephants and astonished at the elephants' ability to work with men. They saw elephants lifting huge logs that would normally have needed several men to move.

"Look at him work!" Frank marveled. "He can do the work of both horses and men!"

"True," Albert said. "But, I can imagine how much he must eat, and I don't want to be the one shoveling his stall! Besides, where would we get his snow boots?" Everyone laughed.

The circus comes to Rockville. Courtesy of the Parke County Historical Society

When no one was around, Wallace and Horace would sneak down to the Coxville covered bridge and climb up to the roof. They would take sticks and pretend they were on a tightrope and walk the peak of the roof line like trapeze artists they had seen at the Chautauqua, bowing and waving to an imaginary crowd. It was a punishable offense when they were caught, receiving lectures on the foolishness of their behavior. They had no sense of fear.

"Ladies and gentlemen," Wallace began as Horace balanced on the ridge. "Watch the amazing Horace as he defies gravity and tempts his fate on the high wire! " Horace laughed. He concentrated on trying to keep his balance to the end of the ridge. Successful, he turned to take a bow. Wallace hollered and whistled.

The boys could see a good distance down the valley from the center of the bridge. In mid-summer it was a sea of green. The flood plain might be filled with dark-green corn or ripening hay, and the trees painted the hills with dozens of shades of blue-green to the yellow-green color of a ripe apple. Emerald-colored grass covered the ground

A chariot in the Rockville Circus Parade. Courtesy of the Parke County Historical Society

and the smell of fresh plants filled the air. It was liberating to be higher off the ground than everyone else and exciting to feel like kings of the world!

Wallace loved the trees, plants and creatures. He spent countless hours watching caterpillars and beetles, and listening to the calls of cardinals, robins, towhees and mockingbirds. He grew to know the life cycle of the plants and quickly learned which ones were useful as food or medicine. He became skilled at wild crafting. He knew how to preserve a plant site by leaving enough plants to drop seed for next season. He learned how much root or rhizome was safe to take while still leaving enough to generate new growth.

The Wheat family spent every Sunday at church. Lee was an elder of the congregation as well as the superintendent of township schools. The Wheat boys spent many hours over the years helping to clean and maintain the building. Pastor Ward always delivered sermons that served up a helping of moral responsibility, fear of the Lord, and devotion to Jesus as the path to salvation. On a cold winter's day the lesson could stretch on for more than an hour until even the adults began to twitch

Roseville Schoolhouse, students and faculty, circa 1890. Courtesy of Galloway Photo

in their seats. In summer, folks could barely tolerate twenty minutes in the heat.

Wallace still puzzled over his mother's death and the fact that no one knew how to save her. His father tried to explain to him in an awkward way the dangers that women face when giving birth. It was just a fact of life that giving birth was God's mystery, and, just like Eve, women were made to suffer in childbirth for the fall from grace of mankind. Women devoted their lives to their children, and sometimes that meant their very life. From the time of his mother' death Wallace could not see a pregnant woman without grave concern over her chances to live through childbirth.

The children went to school in Roseville through the eighth grade. Wallace's school years began to open the world of science to him, and he excelled at his lessons. He was sociable enough. It's just that he didn't have a lot of interest in social activities. He found girls to be a puzzle with their frivolous conversations and confusing social games.

He liked two girls as friends—Anna Baldridge and DeElla Brown. Anna's father was Dr. Baldridge. DeElla's father ran the livery in

Coxville. Apart from these, Wallace much preferred his own company or the company of his brothers or other men. Among his classmates were Anna's brother Robert, Jason Fisher, and DeElla's brothers, Friend and Charlie.

Wallace began organizing plant gathering expeditions at age eleven so that his father could spend more time with the crops. Lee was considering selling the store since Albert was finishing high school and would soon attend Indiana State Normal College. Albert talked him out of it until he could finish school, saying that he might come back and take over.

FIVE

"Here is my mark," Frank said with a laugh as he and Wallace carved a new notch in the woodwork to record Wallace's height on his twelfth birthday. "You're never going to make it to here!"

Wallace stood only five feet, seven inches tall, but he looked taller because he was so lean and muscular. He realized that he would probably never reach Frank's mark at five feet, eleven inches.

"I can hope. I've still got some growing years!" Wallace replied. "Maybe I can stretch myself."

Wheat's store was a busy place in the early 1880s with active mining in the area. By now, most of the men who hung out a medical shingle had at least a year or two of formal schooling in medicine; however, there were still some who called themselves physicians with little or no medical training. Wallace was around to hear some of the conversations that the doctors had with his father about the latest area epidemic, their difficult patients, and what they had found worked well with different ailments.

Albert spent two years at college, but then he decided to go back into retailing. Instead of taking over his father's store, he opened his own store in nearby Mecca Mills in 1882. While Roseville still generated trade with the coal miners and their families, Mecca was the town of the future. Albert thought he could make a go of it there where the population was growing and the prospect of more jobs created a bigger market for his merchandise. He soon built a good trade.

Wallace attended Rockville Normal High School starting in 1884. He stayed with friends of the family during the week, since it was a journey of several miles to school. The roads were always difficult by horse after the snow fell and the terrain was hilly between Roseville and Rockville. He returned to Roseville on weekends to help wait on customers in the store. His senior year in high school was spent at DePauw Preparatory School in Greencastle, along with his friends, Anna Baldridge and DeElla Brown, graduating in 1887.

His older brothers were busy with their lives, and marriage seemed to be on their minds. Albert was the first to marry. He wed Margaret Nielson in 1885. The next year Lee retired from the retail business. He had served as postmaster for 14 years and, also, as Florida Township Trustee for nine years. Now, he just wanted to farm.

Horace had just turned nineteen when he married young Dora King in March 1887. Frank married Ann Craig in August that same year. Both brothers settled near Mecca and continued to work on the farm.

Harvest time, in the fall of 1888, yielded a bumper crop of corn. Some extra workers were hired to help bring in the crop without delay. In mid-September Horace did not show up for work for several days. He was ill, according to Frank. Wallace and his father rode their horses to Mecca to check on him. As they arrived Dora ran out to meet them.

"I'm so glad you're here," she said relieved. "I just don't know what else to do for him. He hasn't been acting right for some time. No appetite to speak of, and he has a headache. He has been complaining about aches and pains for about a week. You know he never does that. He said he was too tired to go to work."

"Take me to him," Lee said. They followed her into the house.

Dora was both exhausted and afraid. She was doing her best to take care of him, but he was very sick. Diarrhea had begun, he had spiked a high fever, and a skin rash had developed. The men immediately isolated him in his bedroom. Lee suspected typhoid fever, based on the descriptions he'd heard from some of the doctors who had visited Chicago during the great typhoid epidemic of 1885.

Wallace stayed by Horace's bedside, replacing cool cloths on his forehead and talking to him. It was known that typhoid was caused by germs that grew in the water or on contaminated food. Horace admitted that he had accepted a ladle of water from one of the farm workers. The worker, being a lazy sort, had filled the bucket from a pool of stagnant water rather than from the water pump. He had shared water with other workers on the farm, many of whom also became ill. Horace had been hit particularly hard.

Wallace stayed with him day and night trying to get him to drink, helping him use the chamber pot, giving him sponge baths throughout the day to combat his high fever, doing all he could to soothe his condition. He felt helpless and angry that there was little one could do to deal with the illness except wait for it to run its course. Dr. Baldridge was called, and he gave him some Baptisia tincture, which was often effective against typhoid, but it was too little, too late. The only hope was that Horace would have the strength to fight through. His fever elevated, and he suffered delirium during the third week of illness. He began to have labored breathing as pneumonia set in.

Wallace fell asleep in a chair beside Horace's bed, exhausted from the ordeal. As the morning sun streamed in the window he woke suddenly, feeling as if something had struck him on the forehead. He shook his head and rubbed his face with his hands to help him wake up. He looked over at Horace. There was no movement. Horace lay breathless and still. It was clear that he had passed, yet Wallace grabbed him by the shoulders and shook him.

"Horace! Horace! Come back! Come back!" Wallace let loose and the body fell back toward the bed. He stood there in shock. A wave of guilt swept over him that he had let Horace die alone while he slept.

Wallace emerged from the bedroom and slowly crossed the dining room to the kitchen where Dora was fixing Lee breakfast. The look on his face told the awful truth.

"He's gone," Wallace blurted out wiping away the tears. "He

stopped breathing. He just stopped breathing. I didn't know. I fell asleep."

Dora began to cry into her dish towel. Lee first grabbed Wallace in an embrace, and then pulled Dora into it as well. Their emotions melded together as they held each other and mourned his passing.

Horace was buried next to his mother in the family plot on the hillside above Roseville. Wallace stood by the grave lost in thought. Why, among all the preparations men had created for disease was there nothing that could save his brother? Wallace was angry and hurt. Who commanded that Horace now give up his life? God? The loss of his closest friend and companion was like tearing off part of his soul.

"Wallace," he heard DeElla gently speak behind him. "Please, come join us at Anna's house. We can all spend some time together."

He turned around. "Thanks, but, I think I would just rather be alone right now. I'll see you later."

He went for a long walk south along the road toward Rosedale and back before rejoining the family to receive mourners and family members at his father's home.

For months after the funeral Wallace buried himself in work around the farm thinking that hard labor might somehow ease the pain he felt. He spent his spare time buried in medical books trying to understand this disease that had taken his brother. Now short-handed on the farm, Wallace didn't enroll in college.

SIX

"Lucy's gonna' have a baby."

Scott stood before his father giving him the news that his girlfriend was pregnant. Lee looked at his son with both disgust and worry, but he did not lose his temper, and he kept the sudden failing he felt as a parent to himself.

He knew that Scott had always had a careless streak. He had a vibrant personality that attracted people to him, but they would soon find out that he had to be the center of attention. Small and not particularly good looking, he always seemed a bit insecure about his place in the world. He liked being the flamboyant one who people could chatter about, and he had an impulsive nature that threw caution to the wind in favor of the thrill of the moment. He was only eighteen, and Lucy was nineteen. There was no honorable course to take other than to offer marriage.

They wed in a small ceremony on Wednesday, September 3rd, 1890. Only immediate family members and a few close friends attended. It was an awkward affair where the bride's condition was becoming obvious, although all did their best to hide the fact that they knew the truth. The couple departed on a happy note for a weekend honeymoon in Chicago. Their first son, Elbert, was born four months later.

The nuptial brought many emotions to the surface for Lee Wheat. He wasn't quite sure why this wedding seemed to trigger all the feelings of loneliness that he held close to the vest. Maybe he was just at that point in life where he felt it was his turn to find some happiness. He had spent thirteen lonely years as a single man trying to raise his family. He didn't want to slip into old age without a partner.

Lee had been courting Adaline Cox of Armiesburg. Adaline's family had been in Parke County about as long as the Wheat family. The two had met while serving on a county prohibition committee. Nineteen years younger than Lee, Adaline was charming and energetic. She made him feel younger and more alive. She was a widow with two children of her own. Lee felt that it was time to propose.

"Adaline, I have been a widower a long time," he began. "Until I met you, I wasn't sure I ever wanted to marry again. I wasn't even sure I could love again."

Adaline looked at him with a smile. She listened intently as Lee tried finding the words to express his feelings.

"I'm quite a bit older than you, I know," he said. "I wondered if we might be happy together, as a couple, I mean. Do you think that might be possible?"

Adaline comprehended his fears quite clearly. She took his hand.

"Lee, we've both known the pain of losing our partner. Please, do not fear that there is not enough love in your heart to want me and to still love Margaret Ann. I would never ask you to choose between us. Just open the door to your heart and make room for one more." She smiled and caressed his cheek.

The family gathered again for Lee and Adaline's wedding on Sunday, October nineteenth. It was a day of celebration, and everyone rejoiced at the union. The women from both families created a simple but lovely wedding for the couple. They made beautiful decorations for the church—paper bells, paper chains, and paper and cloth flowers that were sewn together. They decorated an arch for the ceremony and mixed their crafted creations with fresh greenery and some live flowers from the fields. They put together a lovely bouquet for the bride made of wildflowers, peppermint and fresh leaves tied with ribbon and lace. The couple exchanged simple vows. As the bride and groom kissed and turned to face their friends and family, everyone clapped and cheered. It was a moment of true happiness for all.

The reception took place at her father's farm where there was plenty of space to have a party. Everyone enjoyed cake with ice cream and lemonade at the reception. A small band provided some lively music in an area of the yard that had been set aside for dancing. Paper decorations had been strung on posts around a large square. The band played several lively reels, then a waltz or two, to give the dancers a bit of time to recover and to enjoy a twirl around the dance floor in each other's arms. Lanterns and torches placed about the yard promised to let the festivities go into the night.

Wallace enjoyed himself and took pleasure and satisfaction in his father's happiness. Lee looked joyful, and Wallace wondered if he would ever share that kind of union with someone himself. With his father now married, some of the choices Wallace was considering for his own future would be easier to make.

The next morning the couple left on a trip to Washington, D.C. and Virginia to introduce the bride to family members there. After seeing them off, Wallace headed for the woods where he did his best thinking. He wore a knee-length black coat with big pockets when he went herb gathering. It was the right time of year to dig ginseng, and he found a nice stand of it that day. He loosened the dirt around a large plant so that he could pull out the entire root without breaking it. The root was a prize specimen with thick bark of yellowish-white coloring and plump flesh. From the rings on the neck it looked to be a five-year-old root. Its shape resembled the body of a man.

Wallace cleaned off the dirt and clipped the leaves. A fine root like that could be sold for export to China for good money. Men had found it useful for many physical conditions, but it was more highly prized by Eastern cultures than in the United States. The American natives had brought the settlers' attention to the root as a remedy for consumption, exhaustion and digestive ailments. It was one of nature's true wonders. He carefully wrapped it in cloth and put it in his pocket. He found several good ginseng roots that day as well as some bloodroot and some nuts. He did a good deal of thinking about his own future, but came to no conclusions about what direction he wanted his life to take.

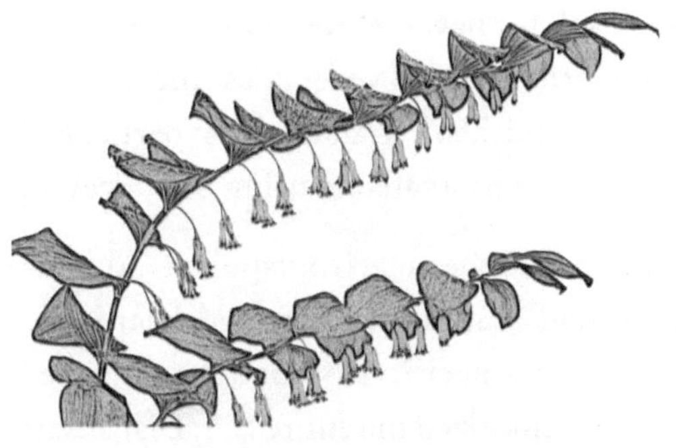

SEVEN

"Colonel, how's the sugar bag supply?" Wallace yelled to Albert who was back in the storeroom.

Wallace helped with the bookkeeping and ordered the groceries and supplies for Albert's store. As an adult he became better acquainted with some of the younger local doctors who would stop in, and he questioned them about their training. Some had as little as six months of formal schooling, although most had attended lecture courses or spent at least a year or two working in a hospital. A growing number had attended medical school in Indianapolis.

It was as easy for a person to start practice as a doctor as it was to be a carpenter, miller or store owner. Medical schools were numerous and unregulated. Aware that the reputation of the medical profession was injured by those who practiced with very limited skills, the American Medical Association (AMA), an organization that wanted to elevate the requirements needed to practice medicine, was calling upon the schools to stiffen their graduation requirements.

The world of pharmacy was changing as well. Manufacturing

pharmacies had greatly expanded the variety of available plant tinctures. Medicines that sometimes caused fatal side effects outraged patients and sent physicians to look for new methods of treatment. These pharmacies isolated the active principles in vegetables and created new formulas with these useful botanicals. Wallace was particularly interested in some of the new treatments available using botanical medicine.

John Uri Lloyd had been an outspoken advocate of botanical medicine. Wallace had read about him and heard Dr. Baldridge talk about him as a great pharmacist. He was known as the brilliant, young apprentice who had memorized the entire U.S. Dispensatory and the U.S. Pharmacopeia, listings of all the drug preparations, while he was still a teenager. He had become the manager of H.M. Merrell and Co. at age twenty-two, later turning it into Lloyd Brothers, Pharmacists, Inc. He had been deeply involved with the work of the Eclectic Medical Institute in Cincinnati and had been handpicked by Dr. John King to help develop and to manufacture the formulas created by Dr. John Scudder for the school. Dr. Scudder's formulas for Specific Medicines had been created to administer precise formulas for specific diagnoses. His medicines were popular, not only with Eclectic physicians, but, also with doctors from other medical disciplines. Wallace thought that Lloyd, more than any other manufacturing pharmacist, was on the right track to discover the secrets of pharmaceutical preparations for the human body because of his strong belief in plants as food and as medicine. Dr. Baldridge had shown Wallace some of Lloyd's papers, which spoke of the importance of the individual in choosing the right medicinal preparation for the disease—that no two people were alike. Lloyd wrote about the need for freshness and purity in botanical preparations. He had pioneered many new combination formulas that were both effective and affordable for the patient. Most of them even tasted palatable when added to juice, much better than some of the wretchedly bitter medicines usually prescribed.

Lloyd also held the belief that the body was capable of healing itself. He wrote that medicines should be aides to natural healing, an idea that

Wallace believed himself. The body knew what to do to correct itself, and the aid of a plant-based medicine could speed the process.

One day, Anna Baldridge invited Wallace over for Sunday dinner with the family. Dr. Baldridge had known Wallace for years and had been a frequent visitor to his father's store. He had received a year of training in medicine at the Eclectic Medical Institute (EMI). Both he and his two half-brothers, John A. and John H. Baldridge, who had also practiced medicine in the Roseville area before moving on to other places, had attended EMI at nearly the same time in the early 1870s. They had all taken an interest in medicine from their father who was a practicing physician in Sullivan County.

While Dr. Baldridge had never claimed any family connections, Wallace had read about Alexander Holmes Baldridge who had been a founder of the American Medical College of Ohio in Cincinnati. He had organized the college to offer an approach to medicine that veered away from the European medical practices of chemical purging, bleeding, and the use of mercury compounds.

His college later merged with the Eclectic Medical Institute, which had been founded by Wooster Beach, a physician schooled in the medical department of the University of New York. He had rebelled against the medical practices of the early 1800s, which included the heavy use of mercury and calomel as curatives. He proposed and practiced the use of medicines that should be given for disease that would act in harmony with nature's attempts to cure, rather than administering substances that were antagonistic. Patients flocked to him in great numbers, more than 2,000 in the first year of his practice.

The word "eclectic", which meant to use whatever treatments had proven useful, seemed to catch fire among these medical practitioners, and came to define their medical methods. These doctors primarily used botanical preparations, but they kept an open mind about anything that proved beneficial to patients. They were willing to accept new ideas, work with what was at hand and built their knowledge of medical practice on the assumption that useful treatments could be found through many means.

Beach opened The New York Medical Academy to teach his methods. A second school was opened in Worthington, Ohio. This school was discontinued after twelve years, and the Eclectic Medical Institute of Cincinnati was organized in 1845.

Wallace joined the Baldridge family for a fine meal of roasted chicken, boiled potatoes and green beans with yellow cake for dessert. After dinner, Dr. Baldridge and Wallace retired to the parlor. Neither man smoked or drank liquor, but they enjoyed a glass of lemonade to top off the meal.

"Wallace, I've known you for a number of years," Dr. Baldridge said as he sipped his drink. "What are your ambitions, son?"

Wallace straightened up in his chair as if to signal the seriousness of what he was about to say.

"I want to study pharmacy, sir. I want to work with John Uri Lloyd in Cincinnati." He searched the doctor's facial expression for approval. Dr. Baldridge quietly contemplated what the young man was telling him. He made no immediate reply but seemed to be measuring the sincerity of the words he heard.

"Wallace, there are not many young men in these parts that I would make this recommendation to, but I think you have both the intelligence and personal characteristics to consider this," Dr. Baldridge began.

"Yes, sir?"

"You know that I attended the Eclectic Medical Institute in Cincinnati," he started.

"Yes, sir. I know."

"It's a fine school, growing better all the time. Actually it is a much better school now than when I attended. They have made great strides in creating a more refined approach to their medical practice. What they teach there is different from what they teach in most of those Eastern medical schools, or even the medical school in Indianapolis. I admire your abilities, son. While I think pharmacy is a growing field, and very important, I just think you should consider medical training. We need a new doctor here in Roseville, someone that the people can trust, someone who wouldn't mind living out here in the country. Have you ever thought about medical school?" Dr. Baldridge queried.

"I have," Wallace replied. "I just was never sure I would like it, being a doctor. I mean, I've met a lot of the doctors around here. Seems like most of them are good people. I just don't know how I'd take to having people's health dependent on me."

"I admit it is not an easy life," Dr. Baldridge mused. "You must be devoted to your patients. You will work at all times of the day and night. You will see disease and death and deformity. But, you will also see life, as you heal, and watch the ill recover because of your skill. You will bring children into the world…it can be very rewarding," the doctor said.

"Eclectics are devoted to being the rural family physicians. We believe in treating patients, not symptoms. I've been practicing for about fifteen years now. I've never been sorry I chose medicine. But, I was old when I started, and I'm slowing down. The people around here need a good doctor who believes in good Eclectic practice. You could be that doctor, Wallace." He spoke so passionately that Wallace was quite carried away by the moment.

"I *will* think about, sir." Wallace's mind was stirring with questions and thoughts about the life of a doctor. "How would I get started?"

"They prefer two years of reading and apprenticeship under an Eclectic physician to qualify for the school. Not every student does this, but it will make you better qualified and give you a chance to see the profession before committing. They don't want you until you have proven an aptitude for medicine and have found a physician who will recommend you. I'm willing to be your mentor if you want to be seriously considered," Dr. Baldridge told him.

Wallace was both flattered and flustered by this proposal. While he thought the science side of medicine would be appealing, being a doctor meant dealing with people in a whole different way. He liked people well enough, but he had always chosen pursuits that didn't make him deal with them on a personal level. Then, he thought about those from his family who had been lost to death or disease. If only a doctor around here had known how to help them, they might have been saved. It could be a profession where he could make a contribution.

"How would I pay for the training apprenticeship?"

"Don't worry about that," Dr. Baldridge said with a smile. "You will be working as my assistant, and you can also do some other things for me, like repairs around the house, taking care of the horses, tending to the garden. I will consider such work in payment. As far as medical school, I would start saving. Perhaps your father can help or give you a loan. We'll figure out that part later."

Wallace spent the whole spring thinking about Dr. Baldridge's proposal. Even then he wasn't sure. Finally, he approached his father to get his opinion. Lee smiled when Wallace told that he was considering medical school. He recalled Mrs. Bynum's prediction for his son at Wallace's birth. Lee assured Wallace that he had the makings of a fine doctor, if that is what he wanted to be. He approved of the apprenticeship and offered to help with the initial finances if Wallace was accepted to the school.

Wallace kept busy working as a farm hand and helping out with the Albert's business. He continued to read and study medicine on his own. He gave a lot of thought to the idea of becoming a doctor. It took him a year to make up his mind, but finally, he went back to Dr. Baldridge, who welcomed him enthusiastically.

DeElla Brown had gone on to college, graduating from DePauw University in the spring of 1894. She began teaching near Coxville the following fall. The next year she became the principal of Rockville High School. Despite quickly rising through the teaching ranks, she soon tired of the job and began to look at other professions. When she heard that Wallace was going to apprentice with Dr. Baldridge, she began to take a serious look at the Eclectic Medical Institute. She approached the two Baldridge brothers who practiced in Rosedale, and they agreed to help her qualify for EMI.

EIGHT

"She can't come in here!" bellowed the Doctor Hamilton's booming voice, forbidding DeElla to enter the treatment room of his office. "Go back to your sewing, woman!"

DeElla stood at the entrance defiant of his command. He slammed the door in her face. Unable to observe the treatment of the patient's wounds, she wandered back outside and sat under a tree until her mentor came out. Dr. John Baldridge was unapologetic for the behavior of his colleague and merely shrugged his shoulders when DeElla protested. He was already taking criticism from his colleagues for taking on a woman apprentice. Much as he believed in her right to learn medicine he felt that he could only push the other physicians so far.

It was an uncommon thing for a woman to want to become a doctor, and even more unusual for her to find a practicing physician who would consent to helping a female. Wallace found DeElla's determination both unusual and somewhat amusing. DeElla never let any man tell her what she could not do with her life. She had spent a great deal of time convincing the Baldridge brothers that she had both the intelligence and the stomach to become a physician. She had more education than both of them, so it was difficult to deny her. DeElla had been attracted to attend the Eclectic Medical Institute both because of their use of botanical medicine and the fact that they were willing to accept women.

All three of their mentors were gentlemen who treated their patients with good humor as they tried to solve the puzzle of ailments presented by their patients. It quickly became apparent to both Wallace and DeElla that medicine involved guesswork as well as skill, and a proper diagnosis was often difficult to make. They carefully watched the diagnostic methods the doctors used, took notes and assisted with treatments when it was requested of them.

It was an eye-opener to both apprentices as they went on house calls to see the way that many people lived. Cleanliness and decent food were not priorities in the lives of many. Mothers knew the practical home remedies of their grandmothers, but there were many things that happened to the human body that did not respond to Grandma's cures.

Contagious diseases would easily spread through an entire household. The apprentices spent a good deal of time trying to educate people about cleanliness as a way of life, which would help stave off diseases caused by filthy conditions or bad water. They discussed the need for clean drinking water drawn from an uncontaminated source, like a good well. They taught people not to eat from the same plate or share a utensil with a sick person, and to wash the sick person's dishes separately from the rest in hot, soapy water. Just these simple measures could be very helpful in preventing the spread of disease.

Some of the most difficult cases had to do lung disease. Doctors attributed many of these illnesses to bad humours in the air. Tuberculosis was one such disease, and it was very difficult to cure. Lung cancer was a death sentence. Those who worked in the mines often succumbed to the dreaded black lung, because they had no protection from breathing in coal dust all day long.

Even when the mines were open, which was only part of the year, coal miners barely made a living. The men would work all day underground in air tainted with the odor of escaping underground gases

Roseville miners with their sons. Courtesy of Galloway Photo

and carbide lamps. At day's end they would come out of the mines covered from head to toe in coal dust. They would scrub themselves down, eat their dinner, and then head out to do some farming or tend to a vegetable patch for their family until there was no longer any light, just to scrape by. Years in the mines would leave their lung capacity depleted and their other organs badly damaged.

The doctor who was called to a mining or farming accident faced traumatic injuries to treat with little in the way of sanitary conditions. Two area doctors handled most of the mining accidents and had heightened skills with severed limbs and head injuries. Once, a miner who had been caught under the wheel of a coal car was brought home in need of a leg amputation. Wallace watched as he was hoisted onto the kitchen table of his home and his leg was sawed off.

Surgeon's kit, circa 1890. Photo by Laura Clavio

One day there was a great deal of commotion outside. Dr. Robert Baldridge looked out the window. Coming toward his office were a group of men with an injured miner on the back of a wagon, his body coated with black coal dust and smeared with blood. He ran out to meet them, and Wallace followed.

"What's happened?" Dr. Baldridge queried the men as he examined the man.

"George was leaning over the side of a coal car leveling out the pile when a big piece of slate fell from the mine ceiling," said Mr. McIntyre. "He was crushed down against the car. I was in another room, and I heard him calling. At first I thought he was talking to someone else, but he just kept on calling. Finally, I went into check on him and found him trapped across the side of the car under the pile. We pulled him out of there and brought him here. What can you do for him? You are the closest place we could bring him for help."

Dr. Baldridge listened intently to the description of what had happened at the Vandalia mine. He looked at the man's back and shoulder. He listened to his chest. The man was badly injured, and his lung seemed to be collapsed. He had little hope that the man could be saved.

"There is not much I can do for him here," Dr. Baldridge told the men. "He needs a surgeon, someone who knows how to deal with these injuries. I'd take him to that new Union Hospital in Terre Haute," Dr. Baldridge advised. He put some dressings on the wounds and gave the man a dose of Morphine to help him deal with the pain. Wallace watched the doctor as the men climbed onto the wagon and disappeared down the road. He seemed distraught. Finally, he looked over at Wallace and shook his head.

"I couldn't help him. I don't have the skill."

He looked Wallace in the eye. "A doctor has to understand his own limitations. I might have tried to do more, but I might have done more harm than good and wasted what precious time that man has left. You must know when to admit a patient's problem is beyond your skill."

Wallace looked at the doctor and thought about it. When should a man say "no" to a challenge? He took the lesson to heart and wondered how he might meet the challenge when he would face it someday in the future.

There were many times when little could be done. A few weeks later, a man who worked at the railway station in Lyford was walking along the top of a boxcar. He lost his balance and fell onto a barrel of acid that had been placed by the side of the tracks. He received severe burns all over his body. Mercifully, he did not last long. There was little anyone could do for him.

Mildred Casey was cooking her family's evening meal on her wood stove when her apron strings caught fire. Before she knew it, her dress was burning, and soon she was engulfed in flames. People kept little water available in the house, and there was no one around to help her. By the time someone saw her she was too badly burned to recover.

Children dealt with a multitude of childhood maladies—scarlet fever, measles, diphtheria, mumps, chicken pox and many unexplained high fevers. Little was understood about the causes of disease. Doctors used common sense practices to keep a child quiet and at rest until the illness had run its course.

It was no small task that the country doctor was asked to take on as a life's work. Medical schools were right to require someone who sought this as a profession to take a serious look at what they would face as a physician. There were no laws or regulations that kept charlatans from practicing. The need for more formal training was recognized, and universities were beginning to organize their medical training so that the requirements to become a doctor were much more comprehensive and rigorous.

Pharmaceutical firms were also demanding that doctors receive more training and were beginning to work with university partners to create programs of pharmacology training as well. The American Medical Association had begun to gather power, and its members hoped to affect real changes in the medical profession.

One day DeElla and Wallace were invited to meet Dr. Ezra R. Baldridge, nephew of their mentors and a recent graduate from the Eclectic Medical Institute, who was setting up a practice in Rosedale. They excitedly quizzed the young doctor about the Cincinnati school and his experiences there. He had married a girl from Cincinnati, so he had close ties to the community as well as to the school. He was happy to regale them with stories about his medical school days and what they would experience. The two students listened intently and anxiously awaited news of their acceptance into EMI. When their letter came, the Brown and Wheat families held a party for them.

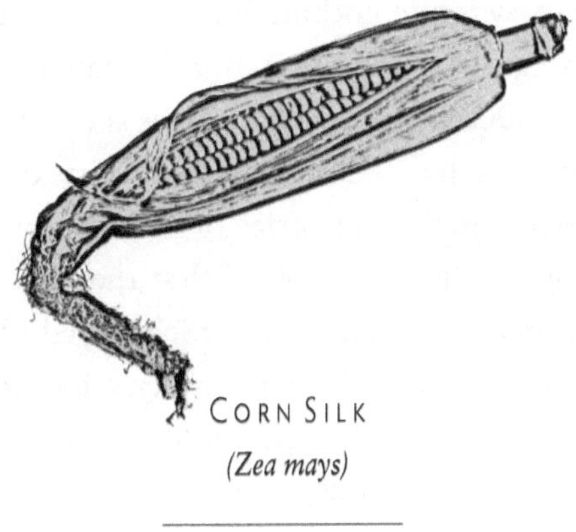

NINE

At last, the day came for Wallace to leave for Cincinnati. It was a Monday in early September. He was leaving for Ohio a week before classes were scheduled to begin so he would have time to get settled. He wanted to see the city, find a decent place to live and become acquainted with the community.

"Take care of yourself, son." Lee embraced Wallace as he prepared to board the train in nearby Montezuma for the trip to Cincinnati.

"Don't let down your guard, big brother!" quipped Scott. "Be wary of those big city women."

Frank looked at Scott and rolled his eyes as he shook Wallace's hand.

"I know you are going to do well," he said. "Come back to us a doctor!"

Wallace jumped on board.

"Good-bye. And, please, write!" Wallace yelled as he waved from the train window.

DeElla's father was accompanying her to school to help her find proper housing. He was concerned that she would not be greeted with open arms by the medical school.

The railway took Wallace to the main station located in the heart of Cincinnati. The city was like nothing Wallace had ever seen before. He had been to Indianapolis many times, but in comparison to Cincinnati, which had over 300,000 people, Indianapolis seemed small. Cincinnati was a river town and had been a gateway city during the western expansion. It thrived on the industries of iron, clothing manufacturing and woodworking. Wallace had heard that they had packed so much hog meat in Cincinnati that it had been nicknamed "Porkopolis" back in the 1830s. It was now 1896, and the city had lost its prominent position in that industry to Chicago. Still, it was a bustling, smoke-filled factory town with dirty, noisy streets, hustlers and factory workers with little to do in their spare time but carouse and drink.

Wallace was met at the train by a small group of upperclassmen from the EMI who immediately grabbed his luggage. They circled him like a flock of buzzards descending upon fresh prey. They straightened his coat, flicked lint from his shoulders and adjusted his hat.

"Ah! An older member of the freshman class to be sure!" said one, sizing up the new matriculant.

"I wonder what he's made of..., " mused another. "He's awfully cute! But, he has a few miles on him. Do you think he will fit in?"

"What do you have to say for yourself, Wheat?" asked another.

Wallace tried to be a good sport about the strange ritual.

"Not much, I'm afraid," Wallace responded. "Glad to be here."

"What kind of name is that anyway, being named after grain?" a short, upperclassman with a dark complexion and wearing a kippot, asked. Wallace just smiled and nodded. He had seen Jewish men before, and he was curious what they were really like. Perhaps now, he would have the chance to find out. He was teased and instructed about what was expected of him as a freshman as the group walked several blocks from the train station to the institute, more than once requiring Wallace to get down on all fours and bark like a dog to show them that he knew his place as a freshman.

Eclectic Medical Institute, Cincinnati, Ohio, circa 1896.
Courtesy Lloyd Library and Museum

The college was in a three-story building at 228 Court Street on the corner of Court and Plum streets. Wallace stood across from the building and stared at the impressive edifice. An eighteen-foot-high Corinthian portico with massive doors decorated the entrance to the building. Tall, impressive glass windows gave the building a sophisticated look. New construction had been attached to the old Eclectic College that had been badly damaged by fire in 1869. The school had been remodeled and expanded around the old structure. On the roof stood a turret, and a gigantic banner with the word "ECLECTIC" on it waved atop a tall flagpole. No one within sight of the building could possibly miss seeing it.

The group pushed Wallace across the street, opened the heavy wooden doors, handed him his luggage, and sent him up a flight of stone steps. In the foyer, he presented himself at the front desk and was given instruction on how he could complete his registration. He was then given a list of boarding house establishments nearby where he could find a room.

Before leaving, Wallace wandered through the building. He peeked in many doorways, anxious to see the facility. On the first floor was the chemical laboratory. The long counters with many work stations were filled with Bunsen burners, mortar and pestles, funnels, test tubes and beakers of all sizes. Shelving ran the whole length of the counters where hundreds of glass bottles filled with chemicals stood waiting for the student to create various compounds. Wallace gasped at the site, excited at the prospect of working with such a vast array of equipment and supplies. He couldn't wait to use it. From there he wandered past faculty offices and climbed the stairs to the second floor.

He found a lecture hall with dozens of rail-backed chairs, all neatly arranged in a semi-circle around a small half-circle platform that held a lectern and a tripod for charts. The back wall was lined with over a dozen portraits of important physicians and faculty associated with the institute. He tried to imagine how the room might look filled with students all anxious to hear a prominent lecturer.

On the third floor he found a steeply-raked amphitheater, with twenty-foot ceilings and long, curved, high-back benches arranged in a close semi-circle around a circular platform. Windows at the front and rear gave light to the room and a large skylight focused its beams on a table at the front of the room. A large lamp hung over the table for additional illumination. A stuffed eagle and stuffed rhesus monkey were mounted on a shelf above the platform. A human skeleton was suspended on a cord from the ceiling. Anatomical charts were mounted on either side of a door where the professor entered from behind the platform. A place for surgical and anatomy lectures, Wallace took a moment to walk around the room to determine the very best place to sit in order to see what he was sure would be fascinating demonstrations.

On the fourth floor he found a large laboratory fitted with big washing sinks and tables. There were rows of white coats on wall hangers and piles of large black rubber gloves in the corner. It didn't take him long to figure out that this was where dissection was done. Down the hall he found a hatchway with a hoisting wheel. It was clear that this is how they pulled the bodies up all these stories out of sight. It was all more than he had ever imagined.

His last stop was the library. His mouth dropped open when he saw the volumes of historical medical texts, journals and botanical collections that Dr. Lloyd continued to amass for the school. Here he hoped to find the answers to the questions of human health that vexed him. Perhaps here he could find the reason for human suffering and become one who could help to eradicate disease.

Wallace took his few possessions and headed toward Vine Street, a bawdy district of town that some compared to Market Street in San Francisco. It catered to lusty pleasures with more than a hundred saloons. There were burlesque theatres, bowling alleys, concert halls, shooting galleries, and brothels, plenty of places for the young medical student to get release from the tensions of his studies. For someone with Wallace's limited social background it was a place of unimaginable wonder as he gazed at the vast mix of people that frequented the many establishments and let go of their inhibitions.

He kept on walking until he came to a quieter side street where he found some of the boarding houses that had been recommended. Already twenty-six years old, he was intent on being a serious student, and he wanted to spend little time involved in the lusty frivolity of the men. He didn't want to seem aloof to his fellow students, but he also didn't want to live someplace that would constantly invite distraction. Besides, he had to be extremely frugal with his money. Medical school took three years of reading medicine and attending lectures at the institute. Lecture fees alone were one hundred fifty dollars! Add to that the cost of books, room and board, transportation, and other expenses, school would cost about $350 a year! Even with his father's help that amount of money was difficult to come by.

The freshman class of 1896 was the largest in the history of the College with seventy-six members. Many of the students at EMI chose to live at the YMCA where a man could find a room, often with a roommate for about three dollars a week. Wallace wanted more privacy. He chose a roomy boarding house on Baker Street. It was a large house with a central living room and an adjacent dining room. He was able to rent a bedroom for $4.00 a week, which included breakfast and dinner. The room wasn't much…a cot, a dresser with a pitcher and wash basin and a small mirror big enough to shave, one small desk with a chair and a rack to hang his clothing. There were four rooms on that floor and four rooms on the floor above. He could get a weekly bath over at the YMCA. The landlady was a widow. She and her two children, a son and a daughter, looked after the boarders.

Wallace allowed himself a couple of days to see Cincinnati before he got down to the task of finding a part time job. That would be all he could handle if he really wanted to devote himself to his studies. He walked down to the river to see the steamboats and the pier teeming with shipping activity. He walked by the beer brewers and the soap making operations. He was especially interested in the factories that made carriages and wagons, and he stopped to talk with the workmen there about their craft and carpentry techniques. He wandered the shopping district where he saw a huge array of clothing, shoes, tackle, furniture and many other manufactured items. It was overwhelming to see the number and selection of goods. Wallace had never imagined that so many options were available. His world had been pretty much limited to what his father had ordered for his store or what he had seen in Indianapolis or Terre Haute.

On Friday, he visited the Lloyd Brothers pharmaceutical facility that was housed in the same building as the Eclectic Medical Institute and applied for work. The Lloyds, who recognized the cost of a medical education, tried to employ a few students. They gave him a job packing plant material into the steam extractors.

Wallace wasn't afraid of hard work, and he was actually thrilled to have the opportunity to see how the herbs were prepared and how the medicinal properties of the plants were extracted on a large scale. He hoped to plant some herb crops on the farm in Roseville someday. This duty also gave him the chance to examine many unfamiliar plants closely and see their leaf and stem structure. He took careful notes about how the steam extractor was prepared and packed.

John Uri Lloyd not only operated a manufacturing pharmacy, he was also deeply involved with both in the administration and development of the medical school. After serving a number of years as a professor and chair of the chemistry and pharmacy departments at EMI, Lloyd had been appointed its president.

Lloyd and John Milton Scudder, along with fellow faculty member John King and four other dedicated faculty members, had devoted their energies to reforming the school and had accomplished great things. They had improved the medical training of the students. They had formulated Specific Diagnosis treatments for many ailments and supported it with Specific Medicines with formulas to treat many disease conditions.

Lloyd's work had brought him to the forefront of the pharmaceutical world as president of the American Pharmaceutical Association. Known for his honesty, integrity and encyclopedic knowledge of his field, Lloyd also served as a special member of the United States Pharmacopoeial Commission of 1890, a group that set national standards for pharmaceuticals.

The freshmen class of seventy-one men and five women gathered in the lecture hall to be greeted by the dean of the institute and to receive orientation. It was clear that the women were not accepted as equals. The prejudice had little to do with their intelligence and much to do with the fact that they wore skirts. Most men felt that a woman's only place in the profession of medicine was as a nurse or a midwife. These women had earned the right to attend this institute by admittance with the same qualifications as the men and by serving the same apprenticeships, but most also needed the additional pull of being the daughter or the relative of an alumnus to be accepted to the school.

The women had to enter and exit the hall a separate way than the men did, and they had their own reception room. Wallace offered to let the women sit with him to provide them a little protection from what he feared might be an uncomfortable situation. He met them as they came in the door and escorted them to their seats.

The women were greeted with whistles, cat calls and false gentlemanly bravado like deep bows which were followed by humping moves as soon as they passed. The men were a crude, unruly lot with no concern for the women's feelings. They kept up the ruckus until a member of the administration called a halt to it. It was uncomfortable indeed to have all those male eyes examining your body instead of paying attention to the officials at the front of the room. The women were very grateful for Wallace's protective stance.

John King Scudder had assumed management of the Eclectic Medical Institute just a few years earlier from his father John Milton Scudder who had been both manager and dean. The Scudder family had been in control of EMI for over thirty years and had turned the institute from a broke and struggling operation into the Eclectic "mother school" which spawned many similar colleges in other states. John Milton Scudder had, over the years, changed the faculty from doctors trained by other colleges to the institute's own graduates, and what was taught now at the institute much more clearly represented the spirit and practice of current American Eclectic movement.

Scudder had modernized the textbooks, and his new line of Specific Medicines moved away from the harsh and bitter medicines of the past. He had gotten the college on solid financial footing and out of debt, made sure the faculty was paid decently and on time, and even turned a profit for the stockholders. His program had turned out hundreds of doctors who practiced all over the United States, but Eclecticism was particularly strong in the Midwest. Now his son had taken his place at the helm as the manager.

John King Scudder chose not to take on the duties of dean as well as manage the school. Instead the board appointed Frederick S. Locke in 1894 to take the academic helm. Dean Locke had been a faculty member at EMI since 1871 and was a favorite among the students. He chaired materia medica, the branch of medical science that deals with the sources, properties, nature and preparation of drugs. He was also the head of therapeutics, the application of remedies to diseases, and he had authored an important textbook.

"Your attention, please! Gentlemen!.....and ladies....," Dean Locke began. The men erupted into chatter again at the mention of their female counterparts.

"Quiet!" Dean Locke pounded on his lectern. "There will be no more disturbances, or I shall clear this room!"

He greeted the young matriculates with a warm welcome and a genuine wish for their success in their studies. He was a quiet man who took his work seriously but also understood the passions of the young. He outlined what the students would be expected to study in the years ahead and the importance of their task both to the school and to humanity.

"You are to be doctors, and you will be qualified doctors, make no mistake about that!" he stated. "This Institute will only confer degrees on those who prove themselves worthy to be called, Physician!"

He spoke of the philosophy and guiding principles of an Eclectic physician and warned them of the opposition that they might confront from doctors of other colleges who practiced allopathic medicine. He pointed out that Eclectic graduates were prepared to be excellent family practitioners; the diagnosis and treatment of disease were the first priority of their education. With that, he dismissed the assembly.

The upperclassmen scooped up the freshman men and swiftly dispatched them to a local drinking establishment for their first hazing. The women were left to themselves, not welcome in the bar.

Wallace was caught up in the moment, and almost succumbed to the temptation to have a drink with his new classmates. But, he was a strong believer in the temperance movement, and he was frankly surprised that more of his classmates did not feel the same. He settled for a sarsaparilla over the jokes made about him by his classmates and a good deal of direct criticism leveled at him for his defense of the women.

"What is it with you, Wheat?" said Wakeman, one of the

upperclassmen. "Do you want us to ostracize you now, before you've even had a week of schooling? Why do you defend the presence of those women?"

Wallace eyed his opponent carefully and tried to craft his words in a form that would not only make his point but also make it clear that he had no fear.

"Mr. Wakeman, I've known Miss Brown since childhood. In fact, she and I apprenticed together. I have no need to question her competence, as you have no need to question my judgment." He stared directly at Wakeman as he spoke with an impish glint of joy at this confrontation sparkling in his eyes. Wakeman came toward him.

"We'll see about that, Wheat!" Wakeman said, as he started to throw a punch. Wallace grabbed his hand and strongly held it suspended in the air as Wakeman reeled with the jolt of this move against his impending blow. Wallace stood there staring the young man down for some time. The upstart was younger and even larger than Wallace, but he had inferior strength. Most of the men were younger than Wallace, a few having come directly to the Eclectic Institute after finishing high school. In truth, some had not even finished high school, but they had managed to pass an entrance exam. Strings had been pulled to get them admitted to EMI. A few had higher education degrees, usually a two-year, pre-medical degree from a college or university. They were drunk with freedom, drunk with alcohol, and drunk with the availability of loose women to please their passions.

It was hard for men in such a euphoric state to take any woman seriously. Wallace knew all the tricks of bravado, having been raised with six brothers. There were no words these young men spoke that he even considered threatening. He finally pushed Wakeman back across the room where he was restrained by his new friends. Wallace raised his glass and said, "To the graduating class of '99! Here, here!!

Wakeman glared at him. The others were forced to acknowledge the toast, breaking the tension and entirely changing the mood of the gathering. Soon everyone had turned to laughter and gaiety.

ACONITE

(Eranthis hyemalis)

TEN

"Mr. Wheat!" Professor Harvey Felter handed back Wallace's anatomy exam paper. "A little more work on the hand bones, Mr. Wheat, but generally an impressive test score."

Wallace scoured the paper to understand his mistakes. His mislabeling of the hand bones had dropped his grade to 92 for the semester. Still, all-in-all, it was not a bad score.

The first year of medical school was especially challenging. Freshmen were tested on many fronts to see if they had the makings of competent doctors. Could they keep up with the scientific class work? Could they master laboratory techniques? The students studied anatomy, botany, chemistry, physiology, materia medica, physics, hygiene and Latin, and had laboratories in chemistry and dissection.

The professors met the bawdy, undisciplined behavior of their students with calm, unerring patience. Command of the classroom atmosphere was imperative, and the professors warned the students that their lack of attention at any time during the hour lecture would cause the professor to leave and never return, resulting in a failing grade for the class.

The freshman hazing at EMI continued. Freshmen were constantly humiliated by upperclassmen, made to stop in the halls and sing spontaneously, brought to their knees and commanded to recite poetry or be grilled with questions.

The dissection room was filled with the smoke of cheap cigars as students tried to combat the stench of the decomposing bodies. It was a stifling atmosphere, and Wallace couldn't wait to leave at the end of each session. He was heading for the door when he heard his name called.

"Wheat!" Wakeman's voice rose above the chatter in the room. The voices grew silent as Wallace stopped near the exit.

"Wheat, what's the hurry! Come back. I want to introduce you to someone."

Wallace slowly turned around. Wakeman was standing by the corpse that, today, had been sliced open to display the intestinal system, its skin still pulled back to either side of its torso revealing the many feet of bowel that fill the lower cavity of the body. Two other upperclassmen were propping up the body in a sitting position, as the intestine spilled out the side where the connective tissue had been cut.

Wallace slowly walked back across the room and stood in front of the cadaver. The gray pallor of the skin and the unpleasant odor of the decomposing body were revolting. One of the upperclassmen lifted the cadaver's right arm from the elbow extending its hand toward Wallace.

"Please, Wheat, be a good fellow and greet today's classroom guest! Please thank him for his contribution to today's lesson. His name is...... Mr....Grosbeak." Snickers erupted from the observers.

All eyes were on Wallace as he listened to the command. It was all he could do to keep from vomiting as he extended his hand to shake the cold and lifeless hand of the corpse and address him in a courteous manner.

"Mr. Grosbeak," he began. At first he let the prank bother him, but as he continued he decided that playing along was the best way to get the whole thing over. He picked up the pace of the conversation and exaggerated his gestures.

"…..a pleasure to make your acquaintance, sir! Thank you for spilling your guts to us today. It has been a most illuminating experience. We will be gossiping about you for some time to come!" The students erupted in laughter.

Wallace put up with it considering it a rite of passage that all students must endure. Wakeman was especially mindful to take after Wallace, but at the same time, demonstrated a modicum of respect born from fear that kept him from overdoing a prank.

Wallace excelled in dissection and anatomy, but he found chemistry and physiology more challenging, even though his interest in chemistry was keen. He was nearly euphoric when he finally held in his hand John Scudder's textbook *Principles of Medicine* and Dr. Lloyd's *Chemistry of Medicine*. It was mind-boggling how many things could go wrong with the human body. He worked very hard, and he absorbed the material quickly. He managed an overall average grade of 84 his first year.

DeElla outdid him with an average grade of 88. Another woman, Louise Eastman, a junior, had taken DeElla and the other new women students under her wing to give them more skills in dealing with the men and to help them survive their years in medical school. She had the ability to make them laugh at their situation by telling funny stories and letting the women share their frustrations in a way that made them feel welcome and supported.

After a few months on the job, the Lloyd brothers determined that Wallace was a good worker and a sober, solid citizen, qualities that the brothers liked. When they learned of his bookkeeping skills he was put in the accounting department where he helped check invoices for ordered materials against what had been received. While he preferred working in the distillery, this job gave him a broader view of the operation. Wallace took the opportunity to learn the business side of pharmaceutical manufacturing. Plant material purchased from different vendors, different fields, or different parts of the country or the world could change the product. He watched how the chemists worked to determine the quality of the plant material. He kept track of the ways that they blended the batches of plants to get the most consistent final product.

Wallace tried to emulate John Uri Lloyd in memorizing as much as he could. He pored over the texts learning all the most important herbs—Aconite, Arnica, Asclepias, Baptisia, Belladonna, Gelsemium, Lobelia, Rhus Tox, Veratrum and many more. He was now glad he had taken Latin in high school. He studied how the medicinal extracts were combined to produce specific effects on specific conditions.

Professor Lloyd was held in high esteem not only by the medical community but also by his employees. He was a small, quiet man, but the power of his intellect and his polite, considerate manner made him welcome and revered in all quarters.

Wallace was disappointed that the Eclectic Medical Institute (EMI) did not have more lab time, but both Dr. John M. Scudder and Dean Locke had agreed that they preferred to present information by lecture and clinical practice rather than by laboratory science. It was a decision that put them at odds with the practice of laboratory research and experimentation being promoted by some leading university medical schools. Medical hope lay on a slide under a microscope these days. Understanding the unseen world was more vital than the school's leaders realized.

Clinical observation took place on a daily basis at Cincinnati Hospital. Students also worked at the dispensary and attended to patients at the nearby 24-bed Seton Hospital run by the Catholic Sisters of Charity. At the college the students watched surgical procedures in the amphitheater. They studied plant species at the herbarium and examined thousands of mycological specimens in Lloyd's collection. They read eclectic, homeopathic and regular medical journals in the library at the college, the public library, and the hospital libraries.

Dr. Rolla Thomas, a distinguished professor who, on the death of Scudder had been put in charge of the school's work in Principles and Practice of Medicine, tried to define more clearly for the EMI students the differences among the three major schools of medical practice currently being taught in the United States. Thomas was known for his speaking ability. He had dark hair and a bushy mustache and mutton chop whiskers. He looked quite distinguished in his dark suit. His dark eyes penetrated the audience sizing up the students. The room fell silent as he began to speak.

"Allopathic medicine, although its practitioners object to such a name, points to the practice of medicine that works at curing a disease by producing effects opposite to those of the disease," he said.

"Homeopathy purports that as medicines give a healthy person certain symptoms, they will cure disease that shows similar symptoms. The Eclectics choose remedies that will aid nature in the removal of disease. While all three schools have many points of agreement in medical practice, our major points of disagreement lie in our material medica, or the way we use drugs and chemistry for medicine, and the administration of remedies for cure. Our preparations, called Specific Medicines, have been formulated from rigid scientific investigation of the specific action of drugs to create direct or specific action in the pathological condition."

Each year brought the students deeper into medical practice and medical sciences. Many students, like DeElla, went home in the summer to apprentice with their mentor and to hold down jobs to earn tuition money. Wallace stayed in Cincinnati and worked at Lloyds. He hoped to absorb enough pharmaceutical training to pass a pharmacist exam in the future. By his second year there, he was getting some time in their analysis laboratory learning the chemical constituents of the botanicals.

The second year of school added physical diagnosis and electro-therapeutics to the curriculum, as well as medical jurisprudence, obstetrics, surgery, eye and ear, nose and throat, operative gynecology, and mental and nerve diseases. Histology, labor, medical practice, pathology, electricity, and venereal disease were studied in year three, along with concentrated reading on medical texts and much more clinical practice.

Wallace managed to beat DeElla's average of 86 their junior year by a point, but she topped him their senior year at 88.4 to his 86.

"DeElla, you have met the challenges of medical school with the strength and aptitude of any man here," Wallace told her.

She laughed.

"Wallace, they all made it sound like it would be an impossible task for a woman! I challenge any one of them to come and be principal of a high school for a year. Then, we will see what these soon-to-be doctors are really made of!"

Wallace received letters regularly from his brothers and his father. War had broken out between the United States and Spain. Teddy Roosevelt and his Rough Riders were the talk of the medical students. It was the summer of 1898 when he read a letter from home:

Dear Wallace,

We are very busy with the farm right now. The corn crop is looking good, and the rain has been adequate this year for a banner yield. Father is expecting a good price for the corn, better than last year. We all miss you here, especially at harvest time when all extra hands are welcome!

I'm sure life in the city is exciting, compared to here, that is, if you ever get away from the hospital and the laboratory. With you and Dayton both gone, we have had to hire some extra men. Albert is ambitiously building a new two-story building in the new part of Mecca thinking that his business will be more profitable there. Such is progress! The new store will also have a basement so he will have a lot more storage. He even has the upstairs fixed up to have plays and musical entertainment. He heard that they may have a telephone in Mecca soon!

Our friend Robert Blake got word that his son John's name was listed in the Cincinnati Enquirer as a soldier who had died down in Porto Rico in a battle. He is writing to the Army to see if it was his son that was killed.

We did have some excitement here. The Coxville baseball team was playing Brazil, and Clayton, the pitcher, was out for some reason. As a substitute they put in this fellow Mordecai Brown from Nyesville who has been playing with the team. Odd thing was he has a deformed hand having lost part of his index finger in the mines. They called him "Three-Finger" and, boy, could he put

Dr. Wallace W. Wheat. Photo courtesy of Galloway Photo

a twist on that ball! The other team didn't have a chance. I don't think Clayton will get his job back soon, as good a pitcher as he is. Course, you know baseball. As soon as someone sees Brown he'll get an offer and be off to other parts. Still, he turned the whole town on its ear. Hundreds of people are coming to the games. Let us hear from you once in awhile. Your brother looks forward to your return.

All good wishes,
Scott

On May 9, 1899, at the invitation of the faculty and senior class, families and friends gathered for the 54th commencement ceremonies of the Eclectic Medical Institute. Robert Baldridge and his wife were Wallace's special guests, as were Drs. John H. and John A. Baldridge, and her parents, for DeElla. Lee and Adaline Wheat, and Scott made the trip by train to take part in this special occasion.

The graduates and guests enjoyed a meal at a fine Cincinnati restaurant before the 8:00 p.m. ceremony and reception at the Scottish Rite Cathedral. After a musical performance by the orchestra, and a prayer from Rev. Goss, Dean Locke addressed the gathering. President Lloyd made some inspiring remarks and then conferred degrees on the seventy-six graduates. A cornet solo to the music "Columbia" followed. Then, Rev. Goss gave the keynote address. After the benediction the ceremony ended with all singing the school song, "E.M.I".

As a gift for their graduation, both Wallace and DeElla received from their parents their own Eclectic medical bag, which included instruments and basic medicines. Their medical school journey was over. Their adventurous lives as doctors were just beginning. DeElla planned to set up practice in Terre Haute following the Baldridge brothers to their new location in a growing city.

Wallace decided to stay on in Cincinnati to continue working for the Lloyd brothers through the summer. He still had full privileges to use the facilities at the college and continued his studies. He had gotten on well in the city. In some ways it was an appealing idea to stay here, but it was always his intention to return to Parke County. He felt he had a duty to those who had helped him. He was now convinced that it was his moral duty and higher calling to give his life to helping others. As a doctor he was convinced that he would be obliged to give his very life for his patients, if that is what it took. He pledged himself to uphold this personal promise, to act and behave in a manner befitting a physician. It was time to go home, and he had no regrets.

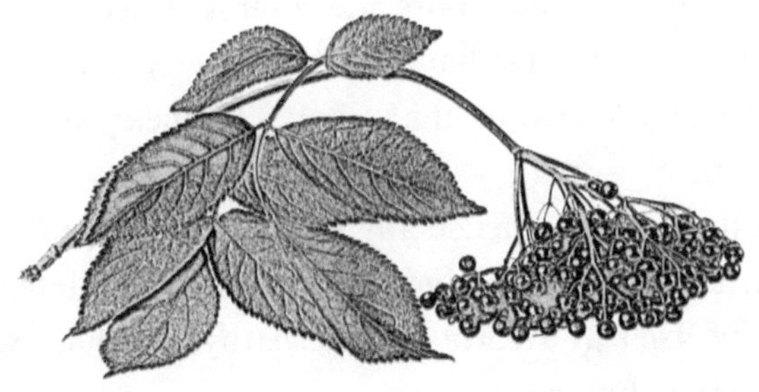

ELEVEN

"What in tarnation is in that box?"

J.M. Snow, a farmer who knew the Wheat family well and had a farm between Mecca and Roseville, received a very large, rectangular crate one day in early September. Wallace had written to him that he was shipping something home and would he please hold onto the crate until he got there?

The box was shaped somewhat like a casket and was heavy. Snow had the delivery men put the crate out in the barn. The weather was hot, and after a couple of days Snow could barely stand to go into the barn because whatever was in that crate stunk to high heaven. He put the crate on a wagon and rolled it out into the yard behind the barn as close to the fence as he could get it, because the smell was upsetting the horses.

Wallace arrived in Mecca with several wooden boxes filled with medical instruments and supplies. He rented a small storefront location on the main street near the covered bridge. Albert had offered him a side room in his store, but Wallace felt he should be on his own. He wanted to establish his own separate identity as a physician. His medical office was fitted with a chair and a table where examinations could take place. On one wall he placed a shelf for a few medical books and put a cabinet with glass doors and several drawers below it to hold his medical instruments. He had another big empty wooden box with a door that he kept loaded on the wagon. The next day he went down to the Snow farm.

"I don't think I ever smelled anything quite that bad! I had to git it outta the barn!" Snow complained to Wallace. He pointed to the crate sitting over by itself in a corner of the barnyard. Flies were buzzing around it in great clusters.

"It's my skeleton," Wallace confessed. "I imagine it's a little ripe. It's still green, and I didn't have time to finish working on it before I had to leave town. I didn't want to leave it behind. Can't get a skeleton on just any street corner, you know," he said, smiling sheepishly.

"Ripe ain't the word for it! Do somethin' with it and git it out of here!" Snow demanded. Wallace thanked him for receiving the shipment. When he opened the crate the stench was unbearable! The barnyard flies started to attack it.

Wallace covered his nose and mouth with a handkerchief and wore rubber gloves as he went to work cutting the remaining connective tissue. He dropped the bones into a big kettle of boiling hot water to clean off the remaining debris. He had to do just a portion of the body at a time in order not to have too big a bone pile to sort out. He took his time and set out the bones in order on an old door—legs, arms, shoulders, hips, spine, skull, all the tiny bones of the feet and hands. Then he reassembled them with glue and wire until he'd rebuilt the skeleton. It took him over two weeks of work.

He carefully laid the skeleton in the big box in his wagon and took it to his office. He hung the skeleton from a hook in the much nicer wooden cabinet that he had brought from Cincinnati and positioned it on the wall at the other end of the room from the instrument cabinet. It would be a useful tool for study and to explain to patients about troubles inside their bodies.

Wallace agreed with Albert that Mecca was a good place to start practice. The town was growing rapidly with over a thousand residents, and it had become the center for business and commerce in southern Parke County. The discovery of rich clay deposits fit for making sewer pipe, drain pipe, building blocks and bricks had attracted the attention of a manufacturer that was building a factory in town that would employ many men. There would be real need for a doctor.

Wallace set up a soda shop in the storefront to help bring in a little extra money and to give folks a chance to get acquainted with him. Friendships could be created over soda, and people were always more comfortable when their doctor was also their friend. He shared the Mecca street with some first-class business establishments—A. J. Wolf & Company's general store; the Mecca State Bank; Albert Bradfield's hardware store; J.D. Swaim's grain elevator; Oliver Hixon's general store; G.W. Kinsey's general store and miner's supply; and Fred Lowe, the shoe and boot maker. Henry Jones ran a good restaurant and confectionery, and Mrs. Murphy kept a fine hotel for out-of-town visitors. Mr. Manwarring ran the livery and stable. It was a business district full of life and action.

At first Wallace was busier with the soda fountain than he was with the medical practice. His friendly nature, direct manner and boundless energy attracted folks to visit the business. He kept a few pharmacy and medical supplies and a few everyday goods to keep the flow of people up.

The soda fountain was a favorite place for the youngsters to visit. On Sunday, everyone knew that Dr. Wheat would give a free piece of Kiss Me gum with each penny soda. The Methodist church was just down the street, and as soon as Sunday services were over, the children would run to the shop with their penny for a special treat. About eleven–thirty in the morning their bright little faces would begin peeking through the front door of the store. Wallace was now more affectionately known as "Doc" to friends and family. This moniker of distinction and honor was one that people felt was less formal than "Dr. Wheat" and allowed them to form a closer relationship with him. His many nieces and nephews called him "Uncle Doc". One bright, late spring Sunday he heard a faint knock on the store's open front door.

"Who's there?" Doc called. When no one answered he walked to the front of the store and looked out. There were five children, all about five to seven years-old, lined up against the outer wall.

"Well, look at this!" Doc teased. "And, who do I have the pleasure of meeting today?"

One brave lad stepped forward.

"I'm William, sir!"

"Oh, William! Very nice of you to stop by today!" Doc kneeled down and held out his hand to shake. William politely bowed, and they shook hands. "Who are your friends here, William?"

William pointed at the other children. "That's Hannah, Joe, Raymond, and that's Alice. But, she's not my friend. She's my sister," he blurted out.

"Yes!" Alice chimed in. "And, I don't call him William. I call him Billy."

"I see," Doc said with a chuckle. "Howdy, to you all. Now who wants to come in?"

"I do! I do!" they all yelled at once.

"Well, come on then," Doc said. They all followed him into the store and he seated each at the counter on a wooden stool with long legs. Their feet dangled and danced as they sat on their high perch and warily eyed the distance from the floor to their seat.

"Now what will you have this morning?" Doc asked as he took off his suit coat and donned his official white soda-jerk cap and a white apron. The kids always laughed when they saw him in his soda waiter role, and it tickled Doc to please them. The orders today were three cherry sodas and two root beers. Doc quickly got to work on the orders. He sang silly songs as he worked. The children watched intently as he created their treats before them. They loved to watch the fizzy soda water bubble up in their drinks.

Soon each child was happily sipping away. Doc would entertain them with stories as they drank. When they had finished, Doc reached in his pocket and produced a handful of Kiss Me gum. Each child was given a piece, which they quickly unwrapped and chewed. Doc gently lifted each child from the tall seat.

"Say, have you had a chance to meet my friend, John Gilbert?" The kids looked at him and shook their heads "no".

"Well, he's a very skinny fellow, I have to tell you. He's always hanging around my office in there. In fact, he hides in my closet." The kids stared in wonder.

"He's kind of a scary fellow…. do you want to meet him?" The kids looked at each other and then looked at Doc. They slowly nodded their heads.

"Okay. Follow me, but stay together and be quiet," he instructed them putting his finger to his lips. They all locked hands. Doc led them on tiptoes into his office and stopped in front of the closet. They all gathered 'round. He slowly opened the door and revealed the skeleton hanging on a hook.

"Say, 'Hello' to John Gilbert!" he said with a flourish of his arm. All the kids screamed and ran out of the store. Doc smiled. He knew that they would be back next week to do it all over again.

People from the Mecca area began to come to Doc for medical help more frequently as time went by. At first it was for the usual complaints of sour stomach, lung disorders and fevers and to get cuts treated. He used a preparation he called "sore dope" on cuts. If the cut was very deep Doc never sewed them with stitches. He closed them with silk tape, which made for little scarring.

People seemed to like his friendly manner and the fact that when they went in for treatment he spent a good deal of time with them. He would talk with them, find out some things about their lives, look at their eyes and their tongues, and then he would make up a medicine just for them. While they didn't especially understand all those bottles of tinctures he had or why he used botanical medications, for the most part they knew what he did for them made them feel better. They just called him an herb doctor. Everyone left with a piece of Haystack chocolate or a fig candy as a little gift. Doc was also prompting them in his own way to start enjoying their way to regularity through eating figs, but he didn't let on.

Mecca's population was growing with more men and their families moving into the area to take advantage of jobs building the new factory. The new shop at the Mecca Clay Works was scheduled to open sometime in 1904. It would employ sixty-five men and house twelve kilns, making it one of the largest clay plants in the world. The kilns at the plant with their round shape and massive chimneys attracted attention from people around the area as a site to see.

Mecca clay works. Courtesy of Terre Haute Star-Tribune

In Mecca, unions ruled the work force. Clay works owner William E. Dee of Chicago also bought the local sewer pipe plant and renamed it the Indiana Sewer Pipe Company. He hoped to double its production capacity within a couple of years. A shortage of available housing delayed the arrival of many families. Men came ahead to start work at the construction site and camped in tents along the creek. Area carpenters were very busy constructing new housing and hoped to have twenty-five houses built before winter would halt the work.

One day, two children came running into the store screaming for Doc to come. A child had fallen off the bridge and was lying in the water. Doc grabbed his medical bag and followed them to where two men were pulling the boy up on shore from the water. He was half drowned and had several broken bones. Doc immediately turned the boy on his side and slapped his back, which caused the child to cough up water and clear his lungs. Slowly he came to consciousness.

"What's your name, son?" Doc asked as he rolled him over until he was flat on his back. His leg was broken below the knee, and his forearm looked as if both bones had snapped probably as he reached out to try and break his fall.

"Daniel, sir," the boy groaned. "Daniel Jones."

"And, how did you fall, son?"

"I was up on the roof of the bridge, sir, and I slipped."

Wallace stopped and looked at the boy. He was lucky that he hadn't broken his neck. Memories of boyhood days when he and Horace walked on the roof of the covered bridge, flooded back into his mind. They had thought themselves indestructible, as he imagined this boy did.

"Well, Daniel Jones, you just lie quiet. You've banged yourself up pretty good here," Doc said softly. The boy looked up at him with a mixture of fear and gratitude in his eyes.

Doc sent the boys who had come for him back to his office for a blanket and some handkerchiefs, and he asked the two men to get a couple of stout branches. They cut down two small trees and with the blanket made a stretcher for the boy. Doc took some small branches and tied them around the boy's broken leg and broken arm with the handkerchiefs to keep them secure.

The men gently carried Daniel back to Doc's office where Doc worked on him for some time. He put a cloth in the boy's mouth for him to bite down, and the two men held the boy as Doc set his bones and bandaged his wounds. Then he made splints for his leg and arm.

The boy's mother was found, and she hurried to Doc's office. He assured the mother that the boy would eventually be all right. He gave her two bottles of medicine, one with Jamaica Dogwood tincture in it for pain, and a bottle with tinctures of Lobelia, Passionflower and

Skullcap to help the boy's muscles relax and help him sleep. The two men helped her get the boy home. The rescue was the talk of the town for the next few days. People were grateful for Doc's quick reaction to the accident and for helping save the boy. Word began to spread about the great new doctor.

BELLADONNA

(Atropa belladonna)

TWELVE

"Scabies, which is commonly called itch, is a buggy vesicular disease of the skin," Wallace said as the introduction of his paper before the Indiana Eclectic Medical Association.

Wallace had energetically set up his practice. He was not only intent on being a good doctor but also on sharing with his colleagues and on participating in the advancement of his profession. He joined the Indiana Eclectic Medical Association as soon as he started practicing medicine. In 1903, he was invited to present his first paper on a medical topic at their annual meeting.

The meeting took place at the Claypool Hotel in downtown Indianapolis with so many Eclectic physicians and their guests attending that the room was overflowing. It was the first time Wallace had been able to present to his Eclectic colleagues as a full-fledged practicing physician, and he relished the opportunity to learn and to share with his fellow doctors from across the state. He had also joined the National Eclectic Medical Association, and he became active in the Parke County Medical Association.

"It is caused by the bug named Acarus scabiei, {and} is contagious by its transmission from one to another. The acarus is a minute round or oval, grayish little fellow, with fine hairs on its head and eight legs projecting from its belly."

Wallace continued, discussing migration of the insect through the skin, living on the adjacent tissues.

"If the male acarus alone enters the skin the disease is not very severe; but if the female is alone, and pregnant, or the male and female enter the skin together, the disease is usually very severe; or if a colony of them enter, it is severe from the fact that they think that the tissues below the dermis are free, and they do not care how much of them they destroy; again, after they are located they attend their church and when they work diligently the disease is more severe; or when they are in the heat of a political battle the disease assumes its severest form and the vesicles run together and form great sores."

He described the fluid-filled vesicles created on the hands and wrist and the itching caused by the busy work of the bugs. He described the differences between scabies, eczema and prurigo and lichen. Then, he summarized treatment options.

"In the treatment of this disease the first thing to be done is to kill the bugs. I have no favorite remedy for this trouble, for when I use my 'favorite' remedy, and think I have the little fellows all killed, they will play 'possum on me, and after a time will be digging away as hard as ever. Sulphur is the old remedy and gives good results; but it is not all; ordinary soft soap is good and if applied to the parts affected will usually destroy the insect. Carbolic acid is an excellent remedy and if applied full strength will destroy big, little, old and young; but I should not recommend it in all cases; only those tough skinned fellows when it is indicated; chlorinated lime, chlorinated soda, oil of cade, oil of turpentine, oil of peppermint and Phytolacca are all good remedies. A mixture of one drachm each of sulphide of calcium and iodide of potassium to two ounces of aqua will destroy the insect; any or all of these drugs will kill the parasite under certain conditions. Unless the clothing is changed sufficiently often a permanent cure cannot be expected."

The congratulations of his colleagues on his presentation gave him the confidence to submit more papers. In January 1904 there was a call for papers for the meeting of the National Eclectic Medical Association which was to be held at the World Exposition in St. Louis, Missouri. It would be the largest ever gathering of Eclectic physicians. Wallace submitted his paper on scabies. He really wanted to attend the meeting, and there was a small stipend for presenters. His paper topic was accepted, quite a feather in his cap, he thought, for a new physician in practice only a few years. It immediately made him a delegate from the Indiana association.

Wallace decided to take the time to really enjoy the experience. He bought a camera so he could bring back photos for everyone to see. He didn't join other Indiana delegates at the train station in Terre Haute for the ride to St. Louis. Instead, he decided to leave a week early and walk all the way to Effingham, Illinois, following the St. Louis, Vandalia and Terre Haute rail tracks and gathered some prairie herbs along the way for his herb collection. In Effingham he caught the train and rode the rest of the way to St. Louis.

One thousand delegates along with five hundred guests came to the national meeting and to enjoy the spectacular exhibition. The National Eclectic Medical Association's thirty-fifth annual convention met for their first session on Tuesday, June 14, at the Epworth Hotel in St. Louis. The Reverend George W. King led the group in prayer. The delegates were welcomed by John I. Martin, a representative of St. Louis Mayor Wells. There had been some discussion among the delegates about the high price of their hotel rooms, which had caught his ear. Mr. Martin assured the group that the rates they were paying were quite common around St. Louis, and everyone applauded.

The members were also welcomed by Dr. J.H. Calloway, who praised the society for the quality of the representatives and the health of the societal organization. He announced that Wednesday had been declared Eclectic Day at the World's Fair and that several committees had been making preparations for it. Everyone cheered.

"Thanks to the hard work of the Reception and Host committee, which is made up of members of the Eclectic Medical Society of St.

Louis," he said, "a banquet will be held tonight on the roof of the hotel with a stunning view of the fairgrounds. And, ladies and gentlemen, you will be among the first to see this fine hotel and our grand fairgrounds enhanced and illuminated by the electric light!"

The assembly clapped and cheered their appreciation. The doctors then got down to the business at hand, the normal reports of such a business meeting, and the presentation of many papers prepared for the convention. Wallace was scheduled to deliver his paper on Thursday to a small group of delegates.

The evening's festivities started with a variety of musical acts in the main hotel lobby and gardens. The doctors enjoyed each other's company and soaked in the exhilarating experience of attending a world's fair. Everyone was dressed in their best clothing for the festive occasion! The scene atop the hotel that night was breathtaking. The delegates, both men and women, and their guests, stared in wonder at the stunning, bird's eye view of thousands of electric lights illuminating the World's Fair buildings nearby.

"How spectacular!" Wallace blurted to all who could hear him. "It's almost like daytime! But, it hides the stars and dims the moon."

For the delegates it was a great opportunity to reconnect with many of their old school chums, to rub elbows with the most famous in their midst and to enjoy a fine hotel restaurant-prepared meal, something rare for many like Wallace who were country doctors.

Association President Joseph L. Hornsby welcomed the delegates and extended the hospitality of the city. Even more Eclectic physicians were expected to arrive tomorrow. A special ribbon for Eclectic Day at the fair had been created. It was passed out to the delegates so that they would be identified as Eclectic physicians and be eligible to receive special discounts and considerations as they wandered the fairgrounds. It was announced that there would be no meeting on Wednesday so that everyone could enjoy the sights and discover the many new inventions displayed at the fair.

The fair had been conceived to celebrate the 100th anniversary of the Louisiana Purchase of 1803. So many states and foreign governments expressed a desire to participate that the date of the fair had to be pushed back a year to give all enough preparation time. On the 1200-acre fairground were fifteen hundred buildings. Wallace had never seen anything so grand as the neoclassical architecture of the exhibition palaces. The Palace of Agriculture by itself covered twenty acres. There were also palaces for themed exhibits in government, education, manufacture, fine art, forestry, fish and game, horticulture, transportation and many others. The Festival Hall contained the largest organ in the world. Some buildings had both heating and air conditioning. One could not see everything there was to see in even a week!

A statue of Saint Louis looked out over the East Lagoon of the grounds. Along "The Pike", a street strip full of entertainment attractions and concessions, there were educational and scientific displays, exhibits of foreign lands, historical displays and theatrical acts. Everyone learned to sing "Meet Me in St Louis, Louis" and danced the two-step to the tune, "On the Pike". Wallace found himself out on the dance floor borrowing the wives of a few colleagues and dancing with a few of the single women, having the time of his life. He turned out to be quite nimble on his feet and quickly caught on to the steps and the rhythm of the music.

For the first time he tasted a newly invented waffle cone made for ice cream, a new drink called Dr. Pepper and a new cereal called puffed wheat. He also tried some foods that were becoming popular in other parts of America—a hot dog, a hamburger, peanut butter, iced tea and cotton candy. He, and most of the others attending the convention, walked to exhaustion trying to take in as much of the fair as possible in one day. It was a wonderland of people, places and things from all over the world, an experience of a lifetime!

The Eclectic physicians found it hard to drag themselves away from the excitement of the fair and back into their meeting on Thursday, but duty called, and they obeyed. Many committee meetings and small group meetings took place on Thursday, discussing scientific updates, treatments and issues in medicine and in the practice of Eclectic medicine.

On Friday, the delegates came together again to create resolutions and policy statements on behalf of the organization. The Association adopted a resolution that firmly put the organization on record as being in favor of the bath for the human animal. It condemned the theory presented in the St. Louis Post-Dispatch by Dr. John Dill Robertson of Chicago that changing one's undergarments was enough to keep the body clean. Dr. Robertson had argued in his article that frequent bathing exposed the body to attack by pneumonia and other diseases. But many Eclectic physicians argued that death rates from pneumonia were much higher than they needed to be because city hospitals spread the disease and city streets needed to be kept clean. The members of the organization argued bitterly over the resolution, but in the end adopted it.

The doctors condemned the use of Morphine or other depressing drugs to treat pneumonia as well as the use of the ice bag to quiet the heart. Many papers were presented, some in small interest groups. Doctor George W. Boskowitz, dean of the Eclectic Medical School in New York, read a paper on "The Therapeutics or Extraordinary Uses of Lobelia" to the whole convention. John Uri Lloyd addressed the group on "Structural Plant Relationship in Therapy and Pharmacy". Doctor Florence Tippet Duval spoke on "Aconite, Belladonna and Capsicum – the ABC of the Eclectic".

The delegates spent additional days at the fair on Saturday and Sunday. Some stayed even longer, but many doctors had to get back to their medical practices and began to depart. The Indiana delegation did not all leave at the same time. Wallace took the train to Terre Haute early Monday morning. His brother Scott met him at the station and took him home. Wallace filled his ear with tales of all the wonderful things he had seen and experienced. Friends and family invited him to a number of dinners so that they could hear of his marvelous adventure and see his photographs.

THIRTEEN

"Leave it behind! The wagon can't hold anymore!" a man yelled at his wife through the pouring rain as she clutched a favorite table in the doorway of their flooding home. "Let's go before the road gets flooded out!"

Spring of 1905 was a season of frequent, heavy rain. It was also a time of great unrest in Mecca as the union workers at Mr. Dee's sewer pipe plant rebelled against what they considered unfair wages. There had been such a long impasse on the issue that many of the striking men had already pulled up stakes and left for other jobs. Nearly fifty families had left town, leaving many empty houses.

Late May and early June saw even more heavy thunderstorms dumping inches of rain at a time. It was so wet that moss was growing in the houses in the hot, steamy weather since nothing could dry out in between storms. The young corn plants now sprouting in the fields would likely be unable to survive as the rain-saturated soil cut off oxygen to their roots.

In mid-June, an even more intense storm came to southern Parke

County, a storm that sat over the area dropping more than nine inches of fresh rain in two day's time. The rushing water was more than the even the broadest banks of Big Raccoon Creek could hold. There wasn't much time to react as rushing water began to fill the streets of Mecca. The panicked residents fled with whatever they could carry or quickly load onto a wagon. Those living in tents hastily abandoned their campsites. The roads soon became rutted, muddy swamps.

Wallace moved as much of his medical practice and store stock as he could to high shelves before he fled to his father's house in Roseville. Lee's house sat far enough back from the creek on the high bank not to be damaged by the flood. The water came all the way up to the bottom of the Roseville Bridge and filled the flood plain to the east.

About a week later, after the flood waters had subsided, Wallace stood peering into the front door of his office. Half the front porch had been torn away by the raging torrent. Inside, the floor was covered with mud. The building would need major repairs. He was unsure if the building owner would even want to repair it.

"Quite a mess, ain't it, Doc?" Wallace heard a familiar voice behind him. It was Mr. Dee greeting him from the street, his clothing spattered with mud, his pants legs tucked inside his boots. His teeth bit down on a big cigar, and he squinted in the bright sunlight as he shielded them with his hand and tried to peer inside Doc's office. He was a small muscular fellow who had learned early on in life that strength of will and determination far outweighed physical stature in the long run. He was a gritty, self-made man with big ideas and the business acumen to make them happen.

"It is, for a fact, Mr. Dee," Doc replied. "What about the plant?"

"I'm afraid we're going to have to shut down for awhile," Dee reported. "I'm not sure what I can save. We've got a huge clean up job ahead. The motors are full of mud and the floor will have to be shoveled out. What's worse is I don't have any workers. The union has cut me off, and the men have walked out on me."

"What? Are they crazy?" Doc asked as he stepped to the front of the porch. "Putting all those families out of work? That's preposterous!"

"They all refused to help me save a damn thing," Dee told him.

Mecca bridge. Photo Laura Clavio

"I guess they think that'll whip me, make me come around to their wage demands, but, mark my words, Wheat, I'm not whipped yet. They'll see." He blew smoke out his nose as he spoke, making him look like a steaming devil, tough as nails. It was obvious that he was a man of his word and not afraid to take on the rough, sometimes brutish, union men.

"What are you going to do?" Wallace asked.

"There are hungry men out there," Dee said. "I'll start hiring them foreigners. They want to work, and they'll work for what I pay them. I'm not giving up. You'll see."

He strode off swiftly toward the sewer pipe plant with his head held high, puffing on his cigar, his steps sure and resolute. Doc knew there were hundreds of new immigrants in the area who were more than willing to work for lower wages than the unions were demanding and much more willing to face the risks of working in dangerous places like the mines. Vermillion and Parke counties were full of immigrants from Italy, Albania, Ireland and other European countries. The men were already working the mines in Vermillion County. He was sure that many of them would jump at the chance to get out of those filthy, underground hell holes and work above ground in the sewer plant.

"I reckon' I will," Doc mused as he watched Dee walk out of sight. Then he got to work on the store.

As he walked inside he found very little that he could salvage. His skeleton case was muddy, but otherwise unharmed. He began to scrub the floors and haul out debris, and he thought about what Mecca was going to be like for the next few years. With so many people leaving, perhaps, this was the time for him to do the same. He wanted to go back to Roseville. His father was not in the best of health. He could be of greater assistance to him on the farm if he were closer. This might be the right time to do it. As he sold off the few supplies he had left, he didn't restock. He continued only his medical practice, until he could make the move.

There were a small number of homes and businesses along Yankee Street in Roseville. Lee Wheat's home was the one farthest to the northwest. There was Lee's old store, the school, the church, the Kinsey home, Sally Gregg's place, a tavern and store run by Sally's sister, and the Fisher's store south of the bridge at the base of Coxville Hill. The Acme Sand Glass plant was just a little further south.

There was an empty building that had been the site of several small businesses, a lodge hall and a saloon over the years. It had once been a two-story building, but the bottom story had been torn out and now only what used to be the second story remained. It sat just to the south of the covered bridge very close to its entrance and right next to the east side of the railroad track. It was about 15 feet wide and 30 feet long. There was nothing fancy about the building, just clapboard siding and kind of run down. The area around the office was overgrown with trees and brush that had been well-watered by the creek. Wallace needed a place that was big enough to live in, provide an exam room and store his medicine. He bought the building and began to make plans for his move.

He fixed it up in his spare time. It was an unpretentious office and residence for a man who put little value on personal possessions. There was a door facing northwest and a window on the east side that he could open in summertime for better air circulation through the building. He cut windows and a door on the south side and a window on the west side of the building for more light and air. He divided the interior space into three rooms. The front area was an open floor where he would store barrels of medicine and wine for tinctures. This room was where he would sleep.

Patients would be expected to stay outside or to go shop in one of the general stores while they waited to see him. Doc put a small stove in the examination room for heat in cold weather. The examination room was uncomplicated and undecorated—a large examining table, a couple of chairs and his wooden cabinet with the glass front for his instruments. He brought his skeleton cabinet and his desk, a modest piece of furniture with some small square boxes built in to hold mail and assorted papers.

He put a cook stove in the back room where he would keep his medical preparation table and his few personal belongings. He cooked occasionally, sometimes food for himself; sometimes a medical concoction was prepared. He was a man with simple needs and consistent habits. He didn't fuss over food, just ate what was at hand. He didn't drink coffee and made sure he ate a fig every day. He had one small dresser for his clothing, and to hold a wash basin, pitcher, and mirror. On his preparation table he kept a microscope and many bottles of tinctures, powders and roots, mortar and pestle for grinding and mixing, scissors, gloves and a beaker and glass stirring stick. Outside he cut down brush and created a path down to the creek to make it easy to haul water.

The remodeling work took several months, and it was difficult work in the cold weather of November and December. In early January, 1906, Doc made the move to Roseville. Word had gotten around that Doc was moving back to town, and the residents were happy to have a doctor move closer to them. Dr. Baldridge was getting up in years and was ready to retire. He was happy to see old friends, but he didn't take any new patients, and he encouraged many to switch to Dr. Wheat.

Adaline Wheat added a woman's touch to Lee's house that made it inviting and comfortable. Wallace had enjoyed coming down from

Mecca to have dinner with them occasionally and to spend some time with his father. While they had always been close, Wallace and Lee had found little time to be together since he had left for Cincinnati years ago. Lee had concentrated on farming for over a decade now and served as the guiding hand for his family, still, as ever, his sons' mentor and confidant, but more philosophical about the meaning and purpose of life. Above all, he valued family and worked throughout his life to keep his family close together and in communication with one another.

It was as if the return of Wallace to Roseville triggered something in the old man's health that caused him to take a turn for the worse. Perhaps it was relief to have him near, or happiness that his son had returned home. Perhaps it was a feeling of satisfaction that what he had set out to do in life he accomplished that may have allowed his mind to accept disease as a prelude to passing. By late February he was bedridden and weak with pneumonia. Doc treated him with Asclepias with a mixture of Aconite and Bryonia and a teaspoonful of Tartar Emetic in water every two hours. He used Podophyllin with salol and bismuth sub-nitrates and gave one powder every four hours followed by a laxative the next day to clean the intestinal system. He greased a flannel cloth with lard and sprinkled it with Lobelia powder to cover the chest and promote warming of the lungs. He kept him on a diet of milk and light broths. Despite Wallace's close attention, he died on March 15th.

The whole community mourned the passing of one of the icons of their town. The funeral was held at the Methodist church, which was packed to overflowing. Wallace had organized the order of the service; but now his thoughts were elsewhere as he mentally reviewed his father's life and the lives of his brothers and their growing families.

Lee had given his all for his family. Wallace still felt that medicine had failed to find answers to turn the tide of disease in so many patients, and he struggled with the fact that he had not been able to do enough to save his own father. He dealt with death regularly; yet, the grief that he felt whenever it was the loss of a family member always served to drive him deeper into medicine and the meaning of life itself, thoughts he shared with no one.

Pastor Ward gave the eulogy. Who better to do so than Lee's best friend and confidant? He spoke with zeal about his friend, their joyous times together celebrating the little landmarks in the lives of his children as they grew and excelled; the sharing of the deep sorrow of losing his wife and a number of children along the way; the joy of remarriage and retirement. His words were meant to soothe the blow of losing this good person and to reassure all that the rewards of heaven awaited a man who had led such a good life. His kind words brought tears to the eyes of most who attended, and the women wailed openly. Wallace listened to the words with a polished note of skepticism. He did not believe anymore that what awaited us on the other side of death's door was a set of pearly gates and eternal rest. There was a guiding source of some kind but there had to be more to life than that.

The six brothers, Albert, Frank, Wallace, Scott, Lee and Dayton, served as pallbearers for the casket. It was loaded onto a wagon, and the funeral procession slowly walked down the road to the other end of Roseville and up Coxville Hill to the cemetery. Friends and acquaintances gathered in silence along the way as a sign of respect. The men then bore the casket to the gravesite. There were only a few families who maintained graves there. Lee was buried next to Margaret Ann beneath a large, finely carved tombstone.

After the graveside prayers Wallace lingered behind as the others left, overseeing the gravediggers and making sure that the casket was secured. Above the sounds of shovels throwing dirt he could hear the sharp, melodic call of the cardinal, a winter bird for Indiana, who now sang a song for a new mate as winter began to lose its grip on the countryside. For Wallace, it sounded like a goodbye song. He saw the first robin of spring. It was an assurance that life always renews itself and that it was the role of nature to recycle everything. He was now an elder of his family, and he felt ready to assume the role.

Edward L. Wheat. center. Photo courtesy of Galloway Photo

Women and man having a picnic. Photo courtesy of Parke County Historical Society

Lobelia

(Lobelia sp.)

FOURTEEN

"Hey! Watch it!" Doc yelled at the driver of a motor car that came barreling down the road nearly hitting him as he walked home with supplies from Fisher's village store. The driver honked at him and didn't stop to apologize. What a waste of time driving was, he thought. All that noise from the engine, the fumes, and the lumpy, uncomfortable seats. He didn't get the attraction. He would take a nice buggy over that any day!

It was good to be back in Roseville. It was home, and he really didn't mind that it was such an out of the way, unexciting place to live. While he had enjoyed the hustle and bustle of Mecca, Roseville would always be his true home. He had plenty of friends and relatives around, although he didn't spend much time with them. He was busy with patients and new responsibilities on the farm. He was never unpleasant and always smiling, but often seemed distant even to people who knew him. His mind was always working on something. He enjoyed the freedom of being in his own practice and not being under the thumb of other physicians or administrators he knew who might disagree with how he chose to practice medicine.

Doctor Wheat in front of the Coxville Bridge.
Courtesy of Galloway Photo and the Parke County Historical Association

He loved the hills and dales of home, the abundant plant-filled woods and the chance to occasionally go squirrel hunting. He kept a .22 caliber rifle in his office for hunting excursions. He enjoyed the soothing gurgle of the creek just outside his door, especially at night when the world was dark and filled with the sound made by crickets.

He was a bit of a night creature himself. He often wandered about in the darkness, and he was fascinated by the star-studded spectacle of the night sky. The thought of what lay beyond this one tiny ball of earth he stood on, in comparison to the vastness of the heavens, was both intriguing and humbling to him. Sometimes, on a moonlit night, he would walk out into the center of a field to get a clearer view of the heavens. It was so exhilarating, he almost felt like a star himself.

The world was his during the night, undisturbed by other humans. It was the time of day he was the most productive and accomplished the most. He needed little sleep. This is when he could concentrate on making his formulas for complicated treatments, mix salves and ointments for skin disorders or do experiments.

He had many new patients. He didn't keep but a few notes on his patients. He wrote notes as long as he was treating them, but he didn't create many formal records. He continued to sit down with patients and just talk with each one to find out something about them—their habits, what they ate and drank, what they did for a living, what they did in their spare time. He would analyze how they looked, the pallor and texture of their skin, the condition of their hair and nails, how the tongue looked, how the eyes looked and a dozen other things he could quickly observe. He would hear their complaints and then figure out a diagnosis and treatment.

Doc would create a medication just for that person by combining tinctures from his many bottles—a drop of this, two or three drops of that, ten drops of something else, until he felt he had come up with the right mixture. The drops were added to a small bottle with a bit of homemade blackberry or elderberry wine that acted as a carrier and made taking bitter tinctures easier.

As an Eclectic physician, he believed in the power of liquid medicine over hard pressed tablets that often didn't dissolve at the right time or passed right through the patient intact. Liquid medication exerted action that conformed close to nature's own method of rejuvenation. He might create pills for someone out of a mixture of powdered preparations and bread. He charged one dollar a visit to see a patient and to provide medicine.

Even early in his career as a doctor he was excellent at diagnosis and was able to help many people. He knew his patients would pay when they could, so he didn't keep much in the way of records of who owed what. He just expected people to honor their debt. Most did. Some would pay with money, some with food or a chicken or some useful item they had, or perhaps by performing a few chores. Those who couldn't pay he just didn't worry about. All the area doctors weren't that loose with their finances. Some would run an ad in the paper when their receivables got too high that would ask folks to come in and settle up their bills. For Wallace, the system worked fine. He had plenty of income, and his needs were few.

Common complaints included: stomach complaints from poor or bad food; constipation; rheumatism and arthritis; lung or breathing complaints; fevers. Some of the most often used tinctures included Lobelia, Aconite, Capsicum, Hydrastis, Podophyllin, Gelsemium, Veratrum, Ipecac, Belladonna, Nux vomica, and Rhus Tox. He had a small book entitled *Index of Diseases and Their Specific Remedies* that gave him a quick primer of the usual tinctures used to treat various diseases that he would then also customize to the patient's specific set of conditions. His success rate in helping people was high. Word spread about his skill and was exaggerated a little more with each telling.

Some of the things he did for people were very simple. For an arthritic farmer's hand, he gave the farmer a couple of buckeyes to roll around in his palm to exercise the fingers. He prescribed a fig a day for constipation, and advised against eating foods from the nightshade family, such as tomatoes, potatoes and peppers. He was always reminding his patients that a good cleaning inside and out was important to health. An herbal tea of chamomile helped some patients sleep. A comfrey leaf poultice was handy for sores, bedsores or bruises. Calendula cream was good for skin problems. Corn silk tea helped ease urinary problems or kidney inflammation. Dried or fresh red clover blossoms steeped in hot water helped menopause.

Of course, there were illnesses that people contracted that no one could help. There were cancers and diseases of the internal organs that could not be seen. He would try to diagnose the cause as closely as possible from the external symptoms. He was straight with patients. He would tell them if he could offer no help or if the disease had a bad prognosis. If he knew of some other doctor who could help, he would refer the patient.

When he was fresh out of medical school, Doc was prone to use more medicines that came prepared by the Lloyd Brothers and other pharmaceutical firms. Every Friday he would make the trip to Bindley's in Terre Haute to pick up tinctures and other preparations. The longer he practiced, the more he came to see an advantage to his patients of using the simplest preparations he could come up with, homegrown if at all possible. The herbs grown closest to the environment where the patient lived seemed to be the most helpful. He hired local people to forage more herbs and roots so he could make a few of his own simple tinctures with alcohol or wine. He liked the freshness of the ingredients and the control that he could exercise over their preparation. He also paid people to gather berries for winemaking. He hired a couple of local women to make the wine.

Disease outbreaks could affect many in the area, such things as scarlet fever, diphtheria, small pox, influenza and consumption. For most, all a doctor could do was provide a bit of medicine, instruct a person's family how best to help the patient, and hope that the person had the strength to survive. A mustard or onion poultice still had use for conditions of cold and congestion.

Babies were being born, and young children had many illnesses to weather. An energetic doctor who could easily travel to attend to these needs was welcomed. Wallace wasn't a miracle worker, at least he didn't think so. He just knew the power of direct medication. He thought some folks heaped a bit too much praise on what he did, but stories of his ability to cure with "herbs" began to spread. Soon people were lining up outside his office waiting for their turn to see him.

Across Yankee Street to the west of his office was the general store that the miners and sand glass quarry workers frequented in the evening to purchase food. They would sit along the creek bank where some of them lived in tents and cook their food. After dark, one might hear the sound of singing or loud conversation as they became drunk with liquor they got from their secret sources.

On the east side of Yankee Street on the north side of the road that led to the bridge was the home of Sarah Gregg. Across Yankee Street to the west lived the Kinsey family. Sarah had been very excited to see the doctor move in. Not only was he a good looking and entertaining neighbor, she saw the potential of profiting from having his medical service in town. She offered him any assistance he might need. Soon she was selling coffee, tea and sandwiches to patients from a small shack that used to serve the railroad while they waited to see him.

Adaline Wheat continued to live in Lee's house and received frequent visits from family and friends. She continued an active social life. Albert sold his Mecca store and moved to Ohio to work for the Hyland Coal Company, but he returned to Terre Haute in 1907 to work as an assistant bookkeeper for Grafe Company. Dayton worked in the mines for awhile, but he soon gave it up to become a jeweler and moved to Indianapolis. Lee, Jr. went to the country of Panama as a bookkeeper on the Panama Canal project. Frank and Scott continued to farm.

The population of Coxville/Roseville rose again as more people came to work in the mines and work at the glass sand plant. The miners were a rough lot. Some were honest working men who, despite their hard labor, received little in salary and could never break the cycle of poverty. Some were immigrants who were working hard and saving their money, living on next to nothing, in order to make it possible for their families to join them from their European homes. Some miners were men who worried about little except the next payday. Their lives were filled with the pain of days of hard work and nights of loneliness. They often caroused to the wee hours of the morning. They would drag their weary bodies back into the mine the next day and repeat the cycle.

There had been much talk among residents about passing laws to prohibit the use of alcohol for the good of all in the area. The Parke County commissioners chose to voluntarily go dry to see if it could reduce alcoholic abuse and make their county a more productive place to live. Those who wanted a drink always seemed to be able to find it despite the ban. Sometimes hiding in vacant buildings to drink resulted in property destruction. So it was for a storage building owned by Adaline Wheat which one day in May 1907 caught fire and burned to the ground.

A couple years later, Adaline moved to a farm five miles west of Rockville. Albert and Margaret decided it was time to move back to Parke County with their family of teenage children. They moved into Lee's big house, and Albert bought into a partnership with the existing general store in town, renaming it Woods and Wheat General Store. The family all enjoyed get-togethers, especially on Labor Day and New

Albert Wheat on left in front of his store. Other man is likely his partner.
Courtesy Galloway Photo

Year's Day, and at the August Chautauqua. Doc enjoyed his family and even though he filled most of his time with his medical practice and his plant experiments, he was willing to take time to be an active part of their activities.

Doc had become especially adept at treating goiter, a low-functioning condition of the thyroid gland. Some of the goiters he saw had grown to as much as eight to twelve inches long. The prominent swelling made a huge bulge in the neck of the patient. He gave the patient an iodine injection directly into the thyroid gland. This was followed with a special root preparation he had concocted. In a week the patient would return and Doc would check the progress. If he didn't feel that there had been enough improvement, he would give a second injection. Generally, two treatments were enough to reverse the condition along with some dietary changes.

He also had special skills with liver and kidney disorders. He put patients on a special diet. No beef or pork. No coffee, tea or alcohol. Eat a special grain that could be purchased from Kellogg's of Battle

Creek, Michigan. Drink lots of water. No peas, no beans. None of that rot gut hooch people were drinking from homemade stills. A fig a day and, then a bottle of his medicine fixed just for the patient, taken half a spoonful twice a day.

Children enjoyed their visits with him. He would laugh and tease them a little and help them relax. He would gain their cooperation with the promise of a treat at the end of the examination, which might be a candied fig or a piece of chocolate. He had a game for such exams, as a look down into the throat cave, thumping their chests to see if there was anything inside there, or a probe into the mysterious ear labyrinth sometimes singing through the examination.

Doc asked area women who wished to work as nurses to check in on patients, change dressings on wounds or tend to a mother after childbirth. Isabelle Terry would make booties for all the babies he delivered.

Doc became so busy with patients at the office that house calls at times had to be limited to the bedfast or a birth. It might be Babe Cottrell, a family member or someone else who was available at the time to drive the buggy for him and tend to the horse. He never knew how long he would have to spend with a patient.

With the county now "dry", the store near the bridge pretended not to sell liquor. Still, men were finding booze and moonshine from hidden sources, and many knew that some businesses were still selling on the sly. Such establishments were nicknamed "blind tigers". The Roseville store was suspected by some to be a blind tiger, but no one had been able to prove it. The proprietor was extremely careful to make her store appear to be obeying the law.

FIFTEEN

By 1910 Roseville had grown in population with miners, farmhands and some factory workers that were employed at the glass sand plant. It had been found that the area around Roseville possessed a very superior grade of glass sand. The quarry supplied the glass sand to The Root Glass Company in Terre Haute. Its combination of elements, including an extremely high level of pyrite, gave glass a slightly greenish color.

The year started off on a sour note with a miner losing his leg at the knee after being run over by a loaded coal car at the mine. Such accidents put everyone on edge. A couple weeks later everyone's mood changed when the C&EI Railroad Company opened the Coxville station, a new stop on the line. There was a short celebration and ribbon cutting at the tracks, but everyone soon dispersed due to the extreme cold of the January day.

Doc enjoyed having Albert and his family back in Coxville. Margaret Wheat was very sociable and was constantly having family members over for visits. The big house bustled with activity. It was a very cold winter that year, and mid-February brought eleven inches of snow in just two days.

Doc still managed to get around to all his appointments. He even made it to Rockville to the annual banquet of the Parke County Medical Society at the Masonic Temple. He enjoyed opportunities to get better acquainted with some of the other area practitioners. Dr. Allen strolled over to the punch table and struck up a conversation with him, while his wife remained occupied in a three-way conversation with other women.

"Dr. Wheat, I have to wonder why the Eclectics stick so passionately to plant medicine. It is unstable, unreliable in strength, and its shelf life is utterly unpredictable. What possible advantage can it have over our newer medicines? Why are you all so stubborn about it?"

Wallace looked at him quietly trying to measure his sincerity. Was he just setting him up for ridicule, or did he really want to better understand his physician's philosophy?

"I beg to differ," Doc said. "I don't know where you obtained your information, sir! Our Specific Medications are quite stable and reliable and made to exacting formulas."

"I just think your physicians would like to keep up with the times," Allen quipped. "There are so many wonderful chemical substitutes, why rely on plants that can have so many variables in strength, let alone, differences in variety and growth variables. Surely you can see the value in that!"

Doc studied his face for a moment.

"Dr. Allen, it is a matter of the living versus the inanimate, if you will. If I take medicinal properties from a plant and convert them into a medicine for a patient, I am taking the strength of one living thing and giving it to another. Is that difficult to understand?"

"On the contrary, Wheat. It is astoundingly simple, even to a fault. You talk as if chemical medicine delivers dead things!" Allen retorted. "Man-made medicines work just as well, and they are far less trouble to produce and cheaper for the patient. You should think about adding them to your pharmaceutical arsenal."

Doc smiled. He had heard the argument before.

"Have you made a study of botanicals, Dr. Allen? I'm not ready to say that I can do better than Mother Nature," he responded. "I still don't know where life comes from, do you? Eclectics just aren't comfortable treating humans with things that totally come from test tubes. A little like playing God, isn't it?"

He strolled away from the punch bowl. Despite the differences that existed among the physicians in their methods of practice, it had been decided by the society long ago to be accepting of all schools of thought. The work of another physician might supply the needed information to treat a suffering patient. Wallace was always congenial with the other physicians but didn't share a great deal about how he treated patients, and he really didn't care to argue the validity of his medical treatments. After all, this was a social occasion.

The tables were decorated quite eloquently with pink carnations, smilax and lighted tapers. Wallace was ever the single man, choosing not to bring a female companion. It was too much trouble. The doctors and their guests enjoyed blue point oysters, olives and pickles for appetizers; a choice of either baked white fish in butter sauce with French fries, or roast chicken with pea patties and potato croquettes; and a Waldorf salad. For dessert, one could choose lemon sherbet or New York ice cream. The doctors enjoyed Coca-Cola or coffee with their cigars at the after dinner smoker and social time. Wallace abstained from both.

By late March, winter began to lose its grip on Roseville. Purple crocus and white snowdrops could be seen popping up from under the leaves, as the sun began to melt away the last snowy reminders of the cold winter months. By the time the woods burst into color in April with trees blooming in white, pink, red and purple blossoms, life seemed to be in upheaval in Roseville. Some say that it must have been the influence of Halley's Comet that made this a pivotal year in the community. Others say it was just life happening.

Late in the afternoon on Saturday, the ninth, John Dorn and Cyrus Shore stood nervously outside the closed door of James Barker's office, the manager of the glass sand plant. Both had been working at the plant for about fourteen months. Shore had decided to quit and had come to collect his pay. Dorn had a pretty good idea of why he had been called there, but he hoped it wasn't what he was expecting.

Barker opened his office door and eyed the two men. His dark, bushy eyebrows almost touched at the bridge of his nose. The bearded, unkempt man had shed his overcoat because the sun was so bright streaming through the bare office window the room had become warm. His rumpled brown trousers were held up with bright red suspenders over a white cotton shirt. He was a heavy man, and he sweat profusely as he held a big cigar between his teeth.

Shore immediately jumped up from the bench when he saw him. Dorn stayed put, his green eyes sizing up the boss. Dorn had a dark complexion with dark hair and a day's stubble on his cheeks. He was lanky and muscular, but thin. In his mid twenties, his face was gaunt and bore the scars of a number of bar brawls. He was dressed in an old plaid shirt and overalls. Shore, a few years younger, had sandy hair and a clean-shaven, boyish look that made him seem less threatening. He wore overalls over an undershirt and had a red bandana tied around his neck.

"Come in, men," Barker grumbled at them. The pair followed Barker into his office and stood in front of his desk. Barker sat down and didn't look up. He reached into his desk drawer and threw a few dollars on the desktop.

"Shore, here's your pay. Not sure why you're leaving, but it's your business. Anything you want to say?" Barker said as he coughed up phlegm from his lungs.

"No, sir," Shore said shaking his head. "I just want to go."

"Okay. Then get on out of here," Barker growled.

"Yes, sir."

Shore grabbed his money and headed for the door. He saluted Barker on his way out and looked at Dorn who returned the look with an expression that reflected a mind filled with malignant thoughts. Dorn then returned his gaze to Barker who finally looked up at him from his desk.

"Dorn, I have to let you go. The supervisor says you been absent, and he can't depend on you. That true?" Barker questioned.

Dorn glared at Barker. "My ma's been sick. She's a widow woman. I had to take care of her."

"You tryin' to tell me you missed work for that, when I hear you were in a brawl just the other night down in Rosedale?"

"I am," Dorn replied defiantly. "Where am I supposed to find other work? The mines ain't hirin' right now, and there ain't no jobs up at the sewer pipe plant neither."

"Well, that's not my problem, is it? I can't help you there," Barker said without much interest. "I got my own troubles. Folks are plantin' right now. Maybe you can find some work in the fields."

Dorn didn't move. Barker studied his face and reached back into his desk drawer and pulled out some more money.

"Here." He put six dollars on the table. "Here's your last week's pay and a week of severance pay. Go on now!"

Dorn glared at Barker as he picked up the money, put it in his pocket and walked out of the office without saying anything else. Shore was outside waiting for him.

"What happened, Dorn?"

"He fired me," Dorn sneered, his eyes darting left and right. "Who needs him."

They walked off a distance from the plant and then lay down near the creek under a large shade tree.

"Why did he fire you?" Shore asked. "I seen you work. You did a decent job in there."

"It don't matter," said Dorn, shaking his head. It was clear to Shore that Dorn wasn't taking this lightly, but then Dorn wasn't sharing what was going on in his head. He just stared at the water.

"Hey, let's head down to the store. We've got money, and I'm hungry," Dorn said.

They walked about a quarter mile up to the tavern store across from the bridge.

The sun was setting, but it was already dark inside the store because the windows were covered with dark cloth. Beulah, the store owner, was putting out cans on a shelf when they came in. She paid little attention to them at first.

"What'll you have?" she asked the pair.

"Well, what do you suggest for a couple of guys who just lost their jobs?" Dorn asked.

Beulah eyed them suspiciously.

"A little down on your luck, hey? You got any money?"

Dorn looked at her with a smirk. "We got some. We just wanna spend it the right way. You know, we kinda' need to drown our sorrows."

"Now, you know we don't sell no liquor," Beulah said eyeing the two suspiciously. "This here's a dry county, at least for now. You wouldn't want me breakin' the law, would you?"

Dorn's face turned dark as anger began to overtake him.

"Come on, Shore, let's get out of here. I thought this might be a friendly place, but I can see that it ain't." He walked toward the door.

"Not so fast," said Beulah, as she raised her hand as a sign that she had something to say.

"I can see that you two ain't had a good day, and, well, I understand that maybe you need to blow off some steam. Now, I can't sell you no liquor, but, I could sell you a 'tonic', you know. Something to treat a bad mood."

Dorn and Shore turned to follow her as she smiled and motioned them to a back room.

"What kinda 'tonic'?" Shore asked.

"The kind that will make you feel good," she said as she reached into a box hidden under some blankets. The unmarked bottles were filled with whiskey.

"Now if you was to buy some 'tonic' for what ails ya', you might just feel a whole lot better."

Dorn and Shore both smiled and nodded their heads in agreement. They left by the back door and took their medicine to the darkening woods in a brown paper bag. By ten o'clock they had finished their medicine. The booze was doing its work, but Dorn wanted more.

Dorn was still angry that he had lost his job and the pair wandered up Coxville Hill cursing and laughing. They visited one of Dorn's friends where they were able to buy a few jars of hooch. They wandered into the Coxville cemetery, thinking that no one would be bothering them there this late at night. They lay on the ground propped up against the gravestones and managed to finish one whole jar of liquor.

"Hey, Shore, I think we ought to show Barker what we think of what he done today!" Dorn said as he fingered the engraving on the stones. Then he jumped up.

"Come with me."

"Where we goin'?" Shore asked as he followed Dorn.

"You'll see..." Dorn laughed. He wobbled as he stood up, put his finger to his lips and signaled Shore to be quiet.

The two walked through the woods down the hill and across the road, then walked along the railroad track spur to the glass sand plant. It was dark, but there was just enough moonlight to see the building. They worked their way closer trying not to be seen or heard by anyone who might be about.

"Gimme your shirt," Dorn commanded in a whisper as they approached the building. Shore stripped it off. Dorn grabbed an oil can from behind the plant building and soaked the shirt with it.

"Hey, what're you doin'? That's my only undershirt," Shore whispered in complaint.

'Quiet!" Dorn said as he sneaked up as close as he could to the building. He stuffed the shirt into one of the empty hooch jars, lit it with a match and launched it up on the roof of the building. The glass shattered and the fire spread out over the boards.

Shore gasped, "What're you doin'?"

"What does it look like? Let's get out of here!" Dorn whispered. The pair ran back up the railroad spur and up into the woods. They climbed a tree and sat hidden by the branches. There, Dorn intended to watch the plant burn.

Wes Moore, the night watchman, was having a cup of coffee up by the gate of the plant when he thought he smelled smoke. He walked around the perimeter to investigate and saw the fire on the roof. He ran back around the front and yelled for help. Before long some men who happened to be on their way home from church up in Coxville came to his aid. They were able to put out the fire before too much damage had been done.

Dorn and Shore who had been muffling laughs now watched in silence. Dorn was decidedly upset that their attempt had failed. They stayed out of sight as the last of the fire was doused with water and the men headed home. Deputy Sheriff Nickles came out to take a look at the damage and search for clues, but it was difficult to see by lantern light. Dorn and Shore stayed hidden watching the action. It would be useless to try to burn it again tonight, Dorn thought.

The two men cut back through the cemetery and then walked down the hill and sat under the covered bridge. They drank some more, and Dorn stewed about what to do. Shore had had enough. He was tired and drunk and ready to go home. But Dorn wouldn't let him go. After all was quiet again, he looked at Shore.

"Come with me," Dorn said as he grabbed the last of the booze.

"Come with you where?" quizzed Shore. "You ain't thinkin' of goin' back to the plant?"

"No," Dorn mused. "No, Somethin' better. Somethin' that will make everyone take notice."

"Dorn, what are you thinkin'?" Shore asked, getting concerned about what Dorn might be planning. "I think we just oughta go home."

"Why? You chicken?" Dorn taunted him.

Shore looked at Dorn and quietly thought about what he might be up to. In truth he was a little spooked by Dorn and a little afraid for his own safety not to appear to go along with whatever Dorn was planning. He was fearful of showing any vulnerability in front of Dorn.

"No, it ain't that. I just think we made our point. Let's go."

"No. You're comin' with me," Dorn insisted grabbing him by his overall straps. "Now come on."

Shore grudgingly followed Dorn into the east end of the covered bridge. Dorn pulled off his own shirt and tore it in half.

"What are you doin'?" Shore asked apprehensively.

"What does it look like I'm doin'?" Dorn replied, smirking

"No. I don't want no part of this!" Shore protested.

Dorn grabbed him by his overalls and pulled him forward.

"What? You gonna tell someone?" Dorn asked. "You're in too deep already."

Shore just stood there afraid to run, afraid to stay.

Dorn grabbed the two remaining jars of hooch and stuffed half the shirt in each. He climbed up into the rafters and placed one jar on top of the support beam. He lit the cloth, then, he jumped down and climbed the other side of the bridge putting the other jar in a similar place and lit it. The dry wood of the bridge roof easily caught the flame. The two men ran across the bridge and up into the woods on the west side of the creek to watch. They climbed up into a tree where they could be well hidden and yet see the whole scene at once.

All of Roseville slept while the bridge slowly burned. It wasn't until about one o'clock in the morning, when the great arches snapped with a loud groan that sounded like a dynamite explosion at the mine, that anyone was aroused. It was all Dorn could do to keep from laughing out loud, proud of his actions and enjoying the sound of the sizzling, crackling wood as it yielded to the flames.

It was Doc who was first awakened from sleep by the noise. He only had to peek out his front door to see the bridge engulfed in flames. He ran out to the road to see what could be done. But, one look at the intense flames told him that it was far too late to do anything but watch the bridge burn. He got as close as he could to try to see if there was anyone in the bridge trapped in the flames. He yelled but heard no reply. Seeing no one, he went back into his office and grabbed his camera. He took a number of photos of the bridge as it burned. He also kept a close eye on his own place, fearful that a spark would jump to his roof.

Others had also heard the noise of the collapsing bridge and had seen the great fire from their front doors. Word spread quickly that the bridge was ablaze. Soon there were dozens of people standing along the road watching.

"What are we supposed to do now?" asked one of the miners. "Are we going to have to swim to work?" Many people around him began to ask the same question. All the mines and many farm fields were up in the hills on the east bank of the creek. The water was deep enough that a person would have to get very wet trying to ford it.

Dorn and Shore had come down out of the tree and joined the crowd by this time, Dorn enjoying the reaction of all the village folk to his prank. His eyes glistened with excitement as he watched the flames.

The Coxville Bridge fire, April, 1910. Photo by Wallace W. Wheat
Courtesy of Galloway Photo and the Parke County Historical Society

Shore was just plain scared and nervously paced among the gawkers. He felt exposed and cold without his shirt.

"I gotta get out of here, Dorn," Shore whispered to him. He started off down the road headed north.

"Pussyfoot," Dorn called after him in a whispered tone. A couple of the miners in the crowd overheard their conversation. Dorn looked at them, kind of stared them down and just chuckled. He had a hard time keeping his eyes off the fire. Still, he was a bit concerned that the miners might be suspicious of him, so when they had turned their attention on another conversation he quietly slipped away and started south down the road toward Rosedale.

Not long after that Deputy Nickles and Jim Lane, who had been deputized to help out since the sheriff was out-of-town, arrived and started to question folks who were watching. It wasn't long before someone mentioned the two young men who had been seen arguing. Nickles began putting two and two together, connecting the incident at the glass sand plant with the burning bridge and surmised that he had a couple of pretty good suspects. Dorn had been seen heading toward Rosedale so Nickles took the car and started that way. Lane took off to the north with the help of another man with a car and soon overtook Shore who offered no resistance.

Dorn had walked about half a mile toward Rosedale when he decided to turn back. He just couldn't resist watching that fire and the anguished faces of the men and women whose lives he had affected. He crossed down to the railroad track and slowly made his way back toward Roseville.

Lane had returned to the bridge with his friend watching Shore who was handcuffed in the back seat. He knew men who loved fire often couldn't stay away. He hopped out of the car and began to walk among the many spectators looking for someone who might match the description that the miners had given him. He was walking down the tree line above the creek looking for clues when he spotted Dorn coming down the tracks. He slowly positioned himself to confront Dorn as he got closer.

"Hey! Hold up there!" he yelled to Dorn. Dorn paid no attention and kept on moving.

"You! Halt! Stop now, son, before I have to lift my gun!" Lane commanded.

By this time Lane had attracted the attention of some of the miners who saw what was happening and began to surround the tracks on either side. At first, Dorn tried to figure a line of escape, but there were too many people around. He'd never get through them. Too many were going to be angry at him if he admitted the crime. He slowed his pace and then stopped to let Lane catch up with him. Doc watched the whole encounter from his front door. His lantern helped light the scene as the men made a circle around Dorn.

"If you're thinkin' I did this, well, I didn't!" he said to Lane.

"Put your hands behind your back," Lane ordered. "We'll talk this over at the jail." He handcuffed Dorn and marched him down the tracks to the car. Dorn caught site of Shore and shot him an accusatory look. Shore responded with a slight shake of the head to let Dorn know that he hadn't given him up. By this time Deputy Nickles, who had not seen Dorn on the road, had returned to the bridge. He and Lane loaded Shore and Dorn into the deputy's car and drove off toward Rockville to the jail.

Some folks stood there to the wee hours of the morning watching the bridge crumble. They eventually all drifted off back to their homes. They would all deal with it when sunrise came.

Doc couldn't sleep. It was hard enough for him to sleep on a quiet night, let alone a night that had held such grave consequences for his little community. There was too much excitement, and the smell of burning wood filled the air. He sat on the ground leaning against the office wall watching the bridge collapse into a pile of charred wood. One man seeking revenge had wrought havoc on the lives of many in this village. How deeply must the anger of many affect us all, he thought.

The next day Doc and his brother Scott were among several men from town who observed the inspection of the damage to the bridge by county officials. Daylight had revealed that there was really nothing that could be done to save the structure. Even the block support footings on either side of the creek were ripped by falling beams, and rebuilding would mean replacing them as well.

"I was at the jail early this morning," Scott told the group. "Those two confessed, although Shore claimed he didn't do any actual burning. More like he was there to watch the whole thing. I believe him. He just hooked up with the wrong fellow. Heard they both had been put out of work at the Acme plant. They confessed to that fire, too."

The men of the village discussed what this was going to do to the town, the farms, and the mines that depended on the bridge for work and commerce. It was clear that everyone was going to be inconvenienced for quite some time.

News spread fast about the fire. Hundreds of people from all over the area began to show up throughout the day to gaze at the damage and gossip with the other folks. There was a lot of discussion about the fact that these two young men had gotten drunk. Where did they get their liquor in a dry county? Who was running the 'blind tiger' or the still that supplied them? Did people really think that closing saloons would just abruptly end the battle against liquor? There was talk of forming law and order leagues to patrol each township to further control alcohol use and catch the lawbreakers. The county couldn't afford more incidents like the burning of the bridge.

About noon Mr. Corey who was a former county commissioner took a look at the damage with Mr. Van Fossen who wanted to be considered as the new bridge builder. They were preparing an estimate for the county.

"Gentlemen, a new bridge is going to cost the county about ten thousand dollars," he informed them. "That's a heap of money for the county to have to pay because of this man's drunken prank. Now, we'll have to take this up with the county council. That takes time. I would say that it will be a couple of months before they will approve it, and then construction will take several months. We'll have to lay a new foundation a little upstream. We will have to make the new bridge a little longer and that will require new abutments."

The timeline led to major grumbling among those present. The mines and much farmland lay on the other side of the creek, and men had to get to work. It was decided that a sturdy rope bridge be strung just a bit upstream so that at least people would have a way of getting across. A committee was formed to approach county government about rebuilding the bridge. Doc was appointed to the committee along with several of the town's businessmen.

The rope bridge was strung upstream a bit from the bridge site. It was three very thick ropes tied together at numerous intervals—one to walk on, two to hold onto as a person tried to balance themselves across. It was difficult to manage, but if someone fell, a person was not likely to drown. Everyone hoped that this spring would not bring high flood waters, always a danger. Some of the men went to work on constructing the rope bridge. Other men and older boys worked to remove the bridge debris from the water and free up the water flow. The charred beams were massive and it took great effort to saw and pull them from the water with ropes and horse teams or tractors.

The new rope bridge had been in use for about two months when a massive June storm swooped in and swelled the waters of the Big Raccoon up to the level where the ropes had been attached to iron posts. The high waters loosened the soil along the banks, eventually pulling the rope contraption from its anchors, and it was swept away. That only raised pressure on the committee and the county commissioners to get a new bridge built. The wheels of county government moved slowly,

A rope bridge across Big Raccoon Creek.
Courtesy of Galloway Photo and the Parke County Historical Society

and some folks felt that because they were in the southern end of the county and not around Rockville that the project was not being given as high a priority as it would have been if they had lived closer to the county seat. Of course, the county commissioners thought that was poppycock. Things just took time.

Some folks took up a collection and managed to come up with

The temporary wooden bridge built across Big Raccoon Creek.
Courtesy of Galloway Photo and the Parke County Historical Society

enough money from members of the community to buy the lumber to build a temporary footbridge. A number of men from the area, both miners and farmers, worked together to build a crude bridge across the creek. It was a big improvement over the rope bridge.

Finally, a contract was granted to Joseph J. Daniels to construct a new bridge. He was to start as soon as he completed construction of the bridge up at Jessup, probably September. Daniels, who was 84-years-old, acted as foreman for the project and chose a new site for the bridge north of the original and went to work hiring some of the local men and bringing in his own crew as well.

The bridge designers first discussed building a concrete bridge instead of another wooden bridge, but the county commissioners considered the cost prohibitive. Jefferson Van Fossen, who was associated with the county road department, was named contractor. The curious were often down by the creek watching the construction. Doc had a front row seat from his office and watched the construction with fascination. The new bridge was footed with sandstone abutments rather than concrete like most of the other new bridges being built in the area. Daniels insisted on

L-R: Edward Fisher, Tom Jacks, James "Jim" Lowe, and the crew boss of
the new Roseville Bridge with the first stone to be laid in the pier foundation.
Courtesy of Galloway Photo and the Parke County Historical Society

Community members remember the bridge building with a photograph.
Courtesy of Galloway Photo and the Parke County Historical Society

Building the new Roseville Bridge.
Photo courtesy of the Parke County Historical Society

stone. This bridge would be longer than the one that burned. The truss was a Burr Arch with two spans. The opening to the bridge was cut in the distinctive arch style that Daniels used on his bridges.

Dorn and Shore were eventually convicted for their crime and sentenced to two to fourteen years in prison. Despite the inconvenience that the whole town had put up with when the old bridge was destroyed, having a new bridge brought new pride and a greater sense of community to the town because of the struggle they had shared together. It was decided by the community to rename the bridge from the Coxville Bridge to the Roseville Bridge, since it really was located in historic Roseville.

C O M F R E Y

(Symphytum officinale)

SIXTEEN

"May we please come to order!" Wallace shouted as he tried to gain the attention of the crowd gathered in the Mecca schoolhouse. "Our first topic for today is scarlet fever…"

Members of the Parke County Medical Association called a town hall meeting one Saturday afternoon in October, as they occasionally did for public service, to help citizens learn more about methods to combat disease. Scarlet fever, measles and diphtheria were reaching epidemic proportions around the state. Doctor Wheat and two colleagues each made a presentation on one of these diseases giving pointers on symptoms, prevention and how to take care of those who became ill. After the meeting adjourned, a woman approached.

"'Doctor Wheat, I'm Louise Delamar. I just wanted to tell you that I found your descriptions of scarlet fever quite accurate," she said. "I recently visited in Chicago where scarlet fever has been raging and found the effects of the disease quite devastating—so many deaths."

Wallace looked up at the sound of her soft, but confident voice. She was beautiful with her dark hair pulled neatly back in a bun and large radiant brown eyes. Her smile was contagious, and Wallace found himself smiling just looking at her. He immediately felt that he wanted to know more about her.

"Miss Delamar, nice to make your acquaintance," Doc said smiling. He was pleasantly surprised to hear a woman who felt confident enough to comment on his presentation. "I don't believe I've ever seen you before," he said.

"Quite right, doctor. I'm the new teacher for the immigrant school that Mr. Dee has opened. He thinks quite highly of you, you know. I came to the meeting this evening to hear what you and your fellow doctors had to say about these dreadful diseases. I'm quite keen to learn more about illnesses the children come down with. I see so many become sick; I wonder how I can help them," she said.

Doc was attracted to her in a way that he had not felt for a woman before, but he was uneasy as he always was around women. He wasn't shy. He just usually didn't pay much attention to women. Louise's smile and her casual conversation made her seem approachable. He boldly asked if he she would join him at table for the dessert and coffee that followed to discuss the topic further. She consented, and, despite the occasional congratulatory interruption by others in attendance, they spent the next hour engaged in a somewhat intellectual conversation about medicine, Homer, Greek philosophy and the effects of prohibition. Doc went home with a strong feeling of expectation that this was a woman with whom he might find many things in common.

It wasn't long before Wallace came to call on Miss Delamar. He invited her for a buggy ride on Sunday afternoon, and they had quite a delightful time riding north of Mecca to his brother Frank's farm for tea and cookies. Frank's wife, Ann, was a generous hostess and made certain that Louise felt at ease visiting with the family. Frank's teenage son, Paul, took care of the buggy and fed the horses.

Before long Doc was making Sunday afternoon a steady appointment, although winter cut down buggy rides. Instead, they would have long discussions on topics they both found interesting. Wallace was surprised at how strongly opinionated Louise could be on such things as the equality of women, the importance of education for all or the importance of being properly fashionable. He felt the need to upgrade his somewhat shabby wardrobe when he was around her.

They might play a board game or a game of cards. It was difficult for Wallace to lose at anything. He was very competitive, but not unpleasant, when he lost a round, except that he might need to take a quick walk to shake it off before he re-engaged in the activity. They enjoyed long conversations on many topics. Wallace was excited to find someone who shared many of his interests.

Louise was both receptive and generous when it came to accepting his less-than-chivalrous ways. Doc was considerate but abrupt. He wasn't used to sharing or not getting his own way. Louise was a match for his aggressiveness, and she did not yield him his way if it wasn't appropriate. Her sharp wits gave her the tools to deal with his intelligence, and he responded to the challenge, having never cared for the kind of women who showed no mental abilities or were only able to flirt.

The two made a handsome couple. Doc was fit and trim and sporting a mustache at present. Louise had strong features and a beautiful, shapely body that she adorned in flattering but practical clothing. She was his opposite with her dark coloring to his sandy hair and blue eyes. She was aware of her beauty and knew how to use it to her advantage. Even so, she often felt that she had to fight with the world of medicine for his attention.

One Sunday in early spring Wallace took Louise to see his office. She was a bit taken back by the way he lived. While it was customary for a bachelor to live simply, Louise was shocked to see the truly Spartan way that he furnished the office and kept his belongings. She wondered why a man of such intelligence and with such a good income would choose to live so humbly.

"Wallace, where do you sleep?" she asked politely.

Wallace looked at her. He normally didn't give much thought to where he slept, if he slept at all. At first he thought her question rather impertinent and personal, but then he realized that a woman always looks at someone's quarters as a home, and it would be a natural concern to her to want to know how he lived.

"I usually sleep over there." He pointed to a place on the floor. Tucked back in the corner was a rolled up blanket and pillow.

"You sleep there?" she said, incredulous to hear that he didn't have a bedroom. She looked at the room crowded with barrels of wine, some coated with dust. The room was hot and vented only by the door and one small window.

"And, what about the kitchen? Where do you eat?" she asked as she surveyed the room.

"Back here," Doc said pointing to the back room. He led her past the examination room and showed her the small room where he kept his medicine and a wood stove.

"I don't really cook much. Sometimes one of the neighbors brings me some food. Sometimes I get something at the grocery. I don't worry about it," he said as a matter of fact. For the first time, he looked around and tried to imagine his home and office through the eyes of someone he was interested in impressing. He had to admit to himself that she might find his lack of concern for his living circumstances and surroundings a little worrisome. He knew what she was doing. They had been seeing each other on a regular basis. She had to wonder if he was a compatible mate. Louise made no comment about what she saw and gave him no clues as to her opinion. She was clever that way. They stayed but a few moments and then left for the rest of their ride.

Despite his infatuation with Louise, Doc never lost focus on his patients or his studies. He saw patients whenever they showed up and then spent the evenings studying, making medicine or engaged in one of his many projects. On the weekends he would make it a point to see her, but the rest of the week was devoted to the practice of medicine or the many other projects that his busy mind wanted to accomplish.

Louise was on his mind all the time. He felt alive in her company. As the weeks went by he began to find more reasons to visit. He set aside some research to make more time to be with her. His depth of feeling was far greater than his ability to express it. These were new feelings for him, powerful feelings that he needed to find a way to understand.

The care of patients was often demanding and challenging. It took more than just an appointment to care for those who had traveled more than a day's journey to seek his help. Goiter patients often stayed a week or two. A number of friends and family members in the area were willing to offer room and board to a patient in a spare bedroom while they received treatment. The locals enjoyed meeting new people and the extra income that renting out a room brought them was welcome.

Louise found it difficult to see him when he was intent on a project, and this perturbed her, but she was busy with her students and had plenty to do during the week. She had to work at getting Doc to be more social and occasionally got him to attend a concert by the local band or the performance of a touring theatrical group. While he was not unhappy to attend such activities, they wouldn't have been something he would likely have done on his own. He realized that a relationship had to include some things that Louise liked as well as what he liked.

No matter what she asked him to do he would put on a smile and cooperate. Louise's friends would often comment on how far she had taken him in integrating him more fully into the community. People were always curious about him, and she was constantly questioned about what he did with all his time and what he was really like—questions she refused to answer.

Many a rendezvous would be interrupted by the urgent need of a patient. If he didn't show up as expected, Louise could only assume that he had been called away. While she hoped to be the center of attention, she was a good sport about it all, and she accepted him for what he was.

The courtship lasted throughout the school year. At the end of the year Louise's school held a ceremony for those children who were graduating. All the parents and many others who worked at Mr. Dee's plants attended the ceremony. All wanted to be supportive of the children. They held a pitch-in supper in the schoolyard. After all the festivities were over, Louise and Wallace went for a walk to enjoy the warming sun and the beautiful spring blossoms. They climbed a big hill to a high spot where they could view the green hills of Raccoon Valley. Wallace was acting a bit nervous.

"Beautiful up here, isn't it?" he said. "I've never seen anything prettier than a sunset over these hills."

Louise looked at him with a raised eyebrow. It was not customary for him to be so poetic.

"You are one of the few men I know who gets excited about leaves unfolding on trees in the spring," she said with a laugh.

"Yes, I suppose that is true," Wallace replied as he kept pacing about.

"Wallace, you seem a bit jumpy this evening. Is something wrong?" Louise asked.

"Wrong? No." he said twisting his hat in his hand. "But, I do have a question." He hesitated looking off into the distance as if seeking verification from something out in the sky that what he was about to do was right. Then he turned toward her, his eyes down.

"Louise, I'm not very good at this. I suppose I should come up with something flowery, but I have never been that way. Well, I just don't know much about that, you see?"

"Wallace, what is it?" she asked smiling and touching his hand. He looked up from the hat and their eyes met. He immediately straightened up, and his usual commanding nature returned.

"Louise, I don't know how else to say it." He dropped his hat, dropped down on one knee and took her hand and looked up at her with pure earnest.

"I think we should get married. I mean, would you consent to marry me? Louise, I love you. I can't imagine going through life without you at my side."

Louise's heart leaped, and she looked down at him. She was at once excited and apprehensive as she looked at his sincere face. Those bright blue eyes seemed to penetrate right through her. He was a man of such character, yet a gem in the rough when it came to handling a woman. She was at once both happy and fearful at the thought of marriage to him, not because she did not love him, but because she knew he would be very difficult to keep up with throughout a lifetime. Still, she knew he was a steadfast man who would likely be there for her always and would love her like no other, and those were qualities that she could warm to with all her heart.

"Wallace. I'm surprised. I was unsure that you wanted to marry," she said.

He stood up.

"Unsure? What does that mean? I mean, yes I do want to marry you. I have thought about it from the first day I met you. I just have been uncertain of myself...of how and when to ask you and whether you would accept me."

He got back down on his knee. He had never been more serious, and had never once been in love with anyone else. He knew that Louise was the one and only love he would ever have. At age forty-one, sixteen years older than she, he was uncertain that she could return his feelings.

"Will you, Louise? Will you marry me?"

Louise looked down at him and laughed and stroked his face. She couldn't resist his exuberance.

"Yes, I will marry you."

Wallace jumped to his feet with a smile that reached from ear to ear. He was like a human spring bouncing about with joy. "Well, fine! That's fine! That's fine! Now, what shall we do?"

Louise laughed. "What do you mean? Don't you want to kiss me?"

"Yes. Yes, of course I do!" he yelled. He engulfed her in his arms and gave her the most passionate kiss of their relationship. Louise was quite overwhelmed. Then he jumped back and began to pace around, his mind bursting with ideas.

"We should have a party, a gathering to make the announcement. What do you think?" he asked.

"I think it's a grand idea," she replied with a smile. Wallace picked her up by the waist and twirled her around, kissing her as he held her in the air. Louise laughed and let herself just enjoy the moment.

"Very well! Let's make our plans for the announcement two weeks from now? We must set a date for the ceremony," he said. He stopped and looked at her. "You are sure? Of course, you realize that you won't be able to teach anymore once we're married."

"Won't be able to teach? What do you mean?" she inquired taken aback by his statement.

"Married women are not allowed to teach in the schools. Surely you know that?" he inquired. "It just wouldn't be proper."

"Not teach!" Louise was surprised by this news. "What shall I do?"

"You shall be my wife!" Wallace said. "Is that so bad? We'll remodel the big house. Albert has taken a new job and will be leaving soon. I'm sure there is much you can attend to there. You shall help me with the practice. I could most certainly use your help. It'll be fine. You will be busy with me and the community."

Louise turned and walked a little way, not wanting Wallace to see the shock and disappointment that registered on her face as she considered the major change this would cause in her life. She had been teaching for nearly seven years and had become very proficient. To have to stop just because she chose to take a husband seemed a waste of her talents. She thought of helping in the medical practice, an idea that did not appeal to her. She could not imagine having to deal with the sick and injured that he saw every day. It was not in her temperament to be patient with such situations. In fact, she feared that the sometimes gruesome realities of medical practice might be completely repulsive to her. Nursing was not like teaching. She really wasn't sure she could warm to the idea of comforting patients.

"Louise?" Wallace called. She did not want to ruin the moment of her engagement, so she put on a smile, turned around and walked toward her intended.

"Wallace, I'm sure we will work everything out. I'm sure of it!" Louise said. They hugged and began their short journey back down the hill to town. Wallace was emotionally on top of the world. His mind raced with joyful thoughts of how he and Louise could build their lives together. He was blissfully unaware of the trepidation Louise felt about the transition for her life. Louise buried her thoughts in her love for this man, and how she could make him happy.

SEVENTEEN

"We offer our hearty congratulations to the loving couple!" Albert led the toast as everyone raised a glass of lemonade and voiced their approval.

The engagement was announced with a small gathering of immediate family and their closest friends at the big house. Doc getting married! It was big news. There was hardly a member of the family that still held out hope that Wallace would ever tie the knot!

A September tenth wedding was planned, a time when the weather was expected to be a bit cooler and the crops were not yet ready for harvest. Wallace had agreed to a church wedding even though he did not attend church. He knew both their families would only feel comfortable with a marriage that had been presided over by a minister. The Wheats were very religious people. Louise's parents lived in Chicago, but they had little family in the United States compared to the Wheats. Her father had been a successful merchant but he was not a wealthy man. Their close friends and family would journey to Mecca for the wedding.

The Wheat women held a shower for the bride. Louise was presented with lovely hand embroidered linens for her dining table. The women enjoyed lemonade and cookies under the shade of a big tree behind Albert's home. Even though Louise had visited the house before she now looked at it as her future home and was making decisions on how she would change it and decorate it.

She was doing her best to understand this collection of women and figure out how she would fit into this family. They were farm women with far more domestic skills than she possessed, or likely ever would. While she preferred a discussion about poetry or books, these women chattered on about every little thing, from the best pie fillings to the latest gossip about the neighbors. They were all so nice to her, yet she had had enough schooling that her interests were far different from theirs. She knew they would more likely judge her on her ability to run a household than her intellectual acumen. Her mother sensed her worry and reassured her that she would fit in just fine.

Louise had been educated at a college for teachers in Chicago. Jobs were scarce there. Mr. Dee knew her father from his days in Chicago. She was teaching in a public school when he suggested to her father that she consider the teaching position at his plant, Louise had jumped at the opportunity to apply for a job outside of the usual public schools. Here, she had more independence in what she taught and how she taught.

Part of her job was to teach the immigrants the American way of life. She had her hands full, not only trying to educate the children in a language that was not their native tongue, but she also had to work with their parents, teaching them the proper things to do as Americans. She tried to help the families divest themselves of the ways of their old world, such as educating the Italians about how harmful eating pasta was to their health. If they wanted to be Americans, then they needed to act like Americans. She found this to be very worthwhile work. Now, she was being asked to give it all up. She wondered if her love for Wallace was strong enough to replace it. She slowly reconciled herself to the coming changes in her life.

In late July, it was time for the annual Chautauqua. This year's list of speakers and activities was quite impressive, and it was an activity that

A Chautauqua parade in Rockville. Courtesy of the Parke County Historical Society

Wallace thoroughly enjoyed each year. He and Louise proudly greeted family and friends on the streets of Rockville as they attended the annual event, which featured entertainment of many kinds from circus acrobats to opera singers to plays. There were also many notable speakers both religious and non-religious that presented new and progressive ideas to the community. There were booths full of useful items, crafts, art and food. They strolled around the streets, and Wallace introduced Louise to many acquaintances and colleagues, sharing with them the news of their upcoming nuptial.

A week later, the oppressive Indiana heat and humidity let up a bit, and a stiff breeze cooled by the waters of the Great Lakes swept across the western part of the state. Wallace and Louise were on their way to a Sunday picnic at a shady spot near the creek. She had packed a wonderful lunch of sandwiches, cake and lemonade. Doc had picked her up in the buggy. They were halfway to their destination when they saw a man on horseback galloping toward them and waving his hat at them.

"What's going on?" Doc mused. He soon saw that it was John Bateman.

"Doc! Thank God I found you!" Bateman blurted out. "Please come with me. Mazey is in labor. It's too soon for that baby to be comin'."

"All right, John. Lead the way. I've got my bag in the back. Louise, I'll have to take you with me for now, understand? There is no time to take you home."

Louise nodded and held on as the horse and buggy dashed over the dirt roads toward the Bateman farm. When they arrived, Doc tied up the horse and immediately grabbed his bag and went inside to see Mrs. Bateman. Louise sat in the buggy thinking that this might not take long. She adjusted her hat and sat primly on the buggy seat. Soon, Wallace came out.

"Louise, I've got to have some help. It is going to have to be you. I've got to have John do something else, and, besides, a husband is usually too nervous and emotional to help. Please come in, will you?"

She looked at him with eyes full of doubt and fear. But, dutifully, she took the hand he offered and stepped down from the buggy.

"Wallace, I don't know what to do."

"Don't worry. I'll show you what to do," he reassured her. "You can start by getting a big pot of water boiling. Take off your hat and gloves and leave them here in the buggy. Thank you for doing this. It may help save Mazey's life."

Louise soon found herself in the kitchen lugging a big pot of water to the stove and stoking the fire. She tied on a cloth to cover her nice dress, but it was soon clear that saving the dress would be hopeless. Doc came out of the room where Mrs. Bateman lay. He poured some of the hot water into a pan, grabbed some cloths from the kitchen and bid Louise to follow him.

As they entered the room Louise saw the amount of blood that the woman had already lost. The stench of blood, urine and mucus filled the air, and Louise gagged. Mazey lay there in pain, a cloth between her teeth to bite down on and muffle the screams. Doc saw that Louise was about to faint, and he grabbed her by the shoulders and held her up. He spoke to her softly.

"Louise, stop for a moment and compose yourself." Louise closed her eyes to get the room to stop spinning. Then she straightened up and nodded to let Doc know that she was all right.

"The baby will be coming soon," Doc told her softly. "It's going to be touch and go. I hope I can save it. I need you to stay with her and tell me if you see the baby coming. I'm going to go outside and mix some medicine for her. Make sure she doesn't push."

Then he was gone. Louise stood there at first looking sick, feeling nauseated, then panic-stricken as she saw him disappear. Then she looked over at Mazey writhing in pain. She walked around the bed and took Mazey's hand just as another contraction came. Mazey pulled down hard on Louise's arm almost knocking her to the floor as she tried to withstand the pain.

When Louise recovered from the lurch she got her footing and sat down on the side of the bed. She spoke softly to the tortured woman.

"Hello, Mazey. My name is Louise. I'm a friend of Doctor Wheat's. I'm here to help you. So, just hold my hand as long as you need to." Mazey looked at her with grateful eyes and nodded then grimaced as another contraction began.

For the next hour Louise stayed there in a contorted position as Mazey hung onto her. She was able to occasionally reach over and get a cool cloth to put on Mazey's forehead. Doc was running in and out of the room making preparations for the birth. He sent John off to recruit a nurse to help. Finally he came in to check on Mazey's progress.

"It's nearly time," Doc said. "Mazey, don't push 'til I tell you to. Hang onto Louise." Mazey was nearly exhausted and her nails dug into Louise's hand. Louise watched in fright as the delivery began.

"All right, Mazey, now push!" Doc commanded. Mazey groaned as her little body bore down and Doc spread her legs even further as she tried to push. She screamed. Her push was weak. Doc took her pulse and her heart was beating slowly, down to about fifty-five beats a minute. He looked at the position of the baby. It was lodged in such a way that it was almost in a breech position. He was fearful that it would come out butt first. He massaged it around with much pain to the mother but managed to move it to where he could see the head. He reached in with the forceps and managed to get hold of the head and gently began to pull.

"Here it comes, Mazey! Push! Here is comes!" Doc yelled. "That's good. That's good!" The baby slipped out of her body. Doc pulled it out and immediately tied and cut the cord and took the baby to a table where he cleaned its air passages and blew some air into its little lungs. It took a couple of halting breaths, then let out a weak cry.

"It's alive, Mazey. He's alive! Mazey, you have a son!" Doc yelled. Mazey smiled but was too weak to make any verbal response. Doc busily rubbed the baby with olive oil and cleaned him off, then wrapped him in a clean swaddling cloth. Mazey had loosened her grip on Louise, and Doc motioned Louise over to the table where he was working on the baby.

"The baby is very weak," he whispered. "It's premature, so its lungs aren't very big. I've got to try to build an incubator to keep it warm. Let me get Mazey taken care of first. Please hold him and make sure he keeps breathing."

Doc put the baby in Louise's arms. She was exhausted. She looked somewhat helplessly at Wallace as if to indicate that she had no idea what to do with a baby. Then she looked down at the little face and couldn't help but bond with him. She carefully took the baby and rocked him in her arms and took him over to show Mazey.

"Look, Mazey. See what you have done? What a beautiful baby boy!" she comforted the ailing mother. Mazey smiled weakly and passed out. Doc worked quickly with her trying to sew up her torn skin and clean up the birth debris. Louise kept a close eye on the child.

Soon after, John arrived back with Sarah Wright to help care for mother and child. Doc related to John what had happened in his absence and the two of them went off to find the supplies needed to build the incubator. Sarah took charge of Mazey, bathing her and doing what she could to freshen the room and bed linens. Louise sat in a rocking chair that John had built for his wife and rocked the child trying to make sure that his mouth stayed clear and he was still breathing. She sang very softly to him.

In an hour the men had returned with a small wooden box that they had crafted, lined with a blanket and a hot water bottle to keep the baby warm. Doc took the child from Louise's arms and laid him in the box atop the warm stove. When he was reasonably certain the child was doing all right, he came over and knelt beside Louise and took her hand.

"Louise, you go rest now. I'll take over. You can't imagine how grateful I am for your help today. We might not have saved the baby's life and Mazey's life without you." Louise was so exhausted all she could do was give a weak smile and stroked his face. What a special man he was and how much everyone needed him.

"John, will you take my buggy and drive her home?" Doc asked.

John consented, and Louise slowly got up and walked to the buggy. She didn't say a word; she didn't know what to say. She was physically drained and emotionally spent. She looked down at her blood-spattered dress. Her gloves and hat in the buggy were the only clean things she had left. The trauma of the event had made a deep impression on her. When she arrived home she pulled off her ruined clothing. After washing herself she fell into bed and slept until time to report to school the next day.

For Doc, the drama of this birth was not nearly over. He knew when a woman had had that kind of trauma in childbirth that her chances of survival were slim at best with a high probability of puerperal fever setting in. While the placenta has been passed without too much difficulty, her uterus was not contracting properly and her pulse was weak and irregular. She had extensive lacerations. Still, he thought he could save her. He began giving her small doses of medicine to help fight what he was sure would be a lot of infection from her wounds, a mixture of Nitro-glycerin, Nux, Cactus, and Coca. He rubbed her with alcohol to stimulate the heart action. She eventually began to stabilize.

It was a fight to keep both mother and child alive through the first few days, and Doc made daily trips there to check on them. Mazey's condition continued to worsen and Sarah alerted him on the fourth day that Mazey was hemorrhaging and passing large clots of blood. The stench from her bedroom, a putrid mixture of blood, pus, dirty linens soaked with bodily fluids combining with humid and hot summer air made an almost unbearable place to be for all concerned.

Doc cauterized her uterus and packed it with sterile gauze and Echinacea tincture mixed into the water for twenty-four hours. He continued small doses of medicine every four hours. After the packing was removed he flushed the uterine cavity with hot saline solution, then with Lysol, and then packed the vagina with antiseptic absorbent cotton. This he did daily until she began to respond and the uterus wall began to contract. He first gave her Cotton Root tincture to control bleeding, followed by Black Haw to continue the treatment. It was fifteen days before her fever broke and signs of recovery became prevalent. Sarah Wright was an extremely capable nurse and looked after her patient diligently, as well as cooked for the men and found a wet nurse for the child.

More than a month later Mazey was finally up and gaining back her strength. Louise did not return to see Mazey again although she knew that folks might expect this of her, having been so intimately involved in the birth. While she admired Wallace for his skill in saving Mazey's life and child, she did not understand how he could deal with such disgusting situations. She set herself to work making plans for the wedding. She had given up her teaching position in anticipation of the marriage, so she desperately needed something to occupy her time.

EIGHTEEN

"Handsome, don't you think?" Wallace asked Scott as they viewed the new buggy in the livery stable. The wedding was just a couple of weeks away when Wallace had his brother Scott drive him in his new touring car to Rockville. He had a special surprise in mind for Louise, a new buggy with rubber tires to bring his bride home.

Scott was amused by it all. He knew that the future was with motor cars, not with the horse and buggy, but he tried to play along with his brother's enthusiasm.

"Beautiful. Wallace, aren't you ever going to get a car? It is 1912. Why haven't you learned to drive yet?" he chided.

"Not interested in cars," Wallace responded resolutely. "I never intend to drive those confounded machines. Too much noise. It scares the horses. Look at this fine leather," he said as he felt the softly padded buggy seat.

"Well," Scott mused, "if you are intent on staying with this old form of transportation, I guess this is as good a ride as you are going to find."

Unidentified man, Jacob A. Fisher, John A. Cottrell, Charles Lambert and
Scott Wheat in Scott's new touring car. Scott's children surround car,
most likely Raymond seated in the tire, Addie Wheat standing,
and Mable and Hazel seated in the background.
Photo courtesy of Galloway Photo and the Parke County Historical Association

Wallace smiled in agreement and called the clerk over to arrange payment and delivery. He didn't want it to come until the day before the wedding, so Louise would not get wind of the surprise.

The women from her family helped sew Louise's wedding dress. Try as she might, she had not been able to get the traumatic experience of the birth of Mazey Bateman's baby out of her mind. Even after she got word that Mazey was going to be all right, the thought of perhaps someday having to go through a similar experience to bear children herself was more than she could reconcile with marriage.

Women who marry will likely bear children and probably many children. How many women lost their lives in childbirth? She didn't care to guess. Was she just afraid? Women have babies all the time and continue to live normal happy lives. Then, along comes someone who has to suffer as Mazey did. As much as she loved children as a teacher, going through such potentially grave danger to have her own seemed a big gamble.

Her doubts went beyond just worries over childbirth. Wallace was a headstrong, brilliant man, very set in his ways and quite a bit older than she. He had a good heart, and he loved her. She knew that. Still, he had unusual ways. He was deeply sensitive, she could tell, but he never let his emotions rule. He never let any situation get the best of him. While he tried to please her and never raised his voice, ultimately, he would want his own way and would more often than not try to persuade her to his advantage until she gave in.

The life of a doctor was all-consuming. The epidemics of cholera, pneumonia, diphtheria, flu or whatever other malady was afoot would often keep him occupied for weeks on end, and she would see him infrequently. She knew that to marry such a man would take an extraordinary amount of strength and perseverance, and she was struggling with herself to accept it even as the wedding day approached.

On September tenth Louise awoke to beautiful blue skies, puffy white fair weather clouds and pleasant temperatures, an ideal day for a wedding! The church was decorated with wildflowers and greenery, and many from Roseville planned to attend the wedding of one of their most famous citizens. The church in Mecca wouldn't be able to hold everyone.

About half an hour before the three o'clock ceremony was scheduled to begin, Wallace showed up in his new buggy. He parked it just past the front entrance of the church, so Louise would be able to see it when she arrived, but where it would not interfere with her entrance. His niece Hazel had decorated it with some white flowers on the side rails and had even made a floral bouquet for the horse's bridle. Wallace was dressed in a fine new black suit, a white shirt and black tie. Albert was to be his best man. Everyone dressed in their Sunday finest and excitement filled the air.

It was soon five until three, and the bride had not arrived. Wallace looked nervously down the road hoping to see the bride's party arriving in her father's car. At three-fifteen people started to fidget in their seats. People in the church began to get up and walk around. They talked quietly among themselves about what might be going on.

By four o'clock, people began to quietly take their leave. Something was definitely wrong, but they didn't want to seem rude or say the wrong thing. Wallace sent Scott to Louise's home to find out where his bride and her family were. He walked down the road a bit, staring at an empty path. By four-thirty everyone except Albert, Frank and Dayton had left. Scott returned to say that he had found no one at Louise's home.

"I looked all over town," he related, "but I didn't see them anywhere. One of the neighbors told me that she saw the family depart in a car and had believed that they were on their way to the wedding, except that Louise wasn't in her wedding dress. She said the car had several suitcases in it. She had just assumed that Louise would be leaving on her honeymoon and that her folks were going home."

"Thanks, Scott," Wallace said. He turned to look at the other men. "Thank you, brothers. Now, if you don't mind, I need some time alone." His brothers expressed their sorrow at this turn of events and left.

Wallace sat down on the steps of the church and thought about what had happened. Why had she left? He couldn't understand what had gone wrong. He had expected this to be the happiest day of his life, and now it was the worst. How could she do this to him? Didn't she realize how much he loved her? How much he needed her? He sat quietly on the church steps hoping that there was some logical explanation and that she would suddenly appear coming swiftly down the road to him.

Eventually he climbed into the buggy and drove slowly home. The clip-clop of the horse hooves was rhythmic with the sorrowful beats of his heart as they sauntered toward Roseville. He was still at the barn when a man drove up in a car with a letter for him. He accepted it and put it in his pocket until he had taken care of his horse. He ambled down the road to his office and took the letter into his back room where he had a lamp. He stared at it for a long time and finally opened it. It was from Louise.

"My Dear Wallace,

At this moment you must be having the most dreadful thoughts about me. I wanted to do my best to explain my actions, although I am sure that whatever I say will not soothe your feelings. I have anguished over this decision for some time, and I am truly ashamed that I could not even find the courage to talk to you in person.

You are the most heroic man that I have ever met. Your life is your work as a physician, and everyone depends on your brilliance and your skill to heal. I have seen you save so many lives. And, I have seen that I am inadequate to deal with what you must do every day. I do not have the heart. I do not have the strength of will or mind to share that burden with you. I would have never guessed this about myself or believed it until events put me to the test.

No matter how much I love you, no matter how much you may love me, medicine will always be first in your life. I understand that. I do. But, I need more, and my need tells me that having to share you with the world this way will leave me feeling bitter and empty. I am not the partner you need. I would not be the kind of wife that could give you the very patient and loving support that a man with your obligations deserves. Nor do I want to stop teaching. I need to teach. I am returning to Chicago with my parents. I hope that someday you can forgive me.

Louise

Wallace leaned back against the wall in his chair contemplating what he had read. He held the letter for a long time as if he could feel Louise through it. Eventually, he folded the letter and put it back in the envelope and put it in his dresser. He contemplated going after her. Maybe he could convince her that life wouldn't be as she imagined, but in the end he let it go.

The next day Wallace drove the buggy down to his office. He parked it and unhitched the horse. He dismantled the buggy piece by piece just like he felt dismantled himself. He reassembled it in the front room of

A Christmas Card Photo of Louise. Photo courtesy of Galloway Photo

his office. There it stayed and often became his bed. He never said a word against Louise or even discussed her, and no one dared bring it up. He never showed anyone her letter. He just bore the hurt without sharing it with even his brothers. He decided that he would never again seek to marry. He vowed to himself never to get so emotionally invested in anyone again. It was too painful. It was too distracting. From then on, he buried himself in the work of medicine.

He had one photo of Louise. It was on a Christmas card. He held it up and stared for a long time at her image as if somehow that would help him read her mind and understand her motives. He tucked it away in the dresser drawer along with his heart.

SLIPPERY ELM

(Ulmus fulva)

NINETEEN

"Quack, quack!" Wallace was mimicking duck calls to persuade some of the ducks he raised to follow him down to the pond when he saw his brother Scott drive by with Stella Carell in his car. Scott didn't see him. He was too busy showing off for his girlfriend.

Scott's family had continued to grow. He and Lucy had six children: Elbert, the oldest was born in 1890. They lost an infant girl in 1893. Dayton, Hazel, Adeline, Raymond all came along, and the youngest, Wallace, had been born in 1908. Scott mostly worked on the farm, and that was always a good excuse to come home late. There was even more temptation after Scott bought the car. He could think of many excuses to be away from home. Then, he met Stella, a young woman nineteen years his junior, and he became deeply infatuated with her.

Just the fact that Scott had the nerve to be seen with her in Roseville was an affront to the whole family. Wallace watched them race by thinking about how he might approach his brother concerning what he feared might be happening. An affair? Well, not a pleasant occurrence at all, but it might still be possible to bring him back to his family. Wallace feared that just a love affair might not be the end of it.

Ducks enjoying the day.
Photo courtesy of the Parke County Historical Society

Scott was forty years old now, a dangerous age for a man who sees his youth and vitality beginning to fall away. The attraction to younger women can be strong. Wallace himself had been attracted to a much younger woman. They respond to the older man because he seems so worldly and mature and generally has more money than the younger men who court them. While divorce wasn't common, it did happen and often had devastating consequences for the spouse left behind.

A few days later Scott stopped by Doc's office in the early evening. The two sat down in some chairs out in the cool night air for a glass of lemonade. Doc broached the subject of Stella with his brother.

"I still love Lucy," he told Wallace, "but, she doesn't excite me anymore. Stella makes me feel alive again, something I haven't felt in a long time. It makes me feel so good, so charged up!"

Wallace watched his brother as he spoke. He could see the spark in his eyes when he spoke of Stella, and he clearly was not thinking about his children or his obligations anymore. He was a man in love, but not with the woman he claimed to be in love with. Doc knew Scott too well to be fooled. He had married so young, and Wallace knew that he had never had the opportunity to stretch his wings and try to fly before the responsibilities of family had come to him through his own carelessness. Now he wanted to find that lost youth in the arms of a new woman where there were no cares or worries.

"Scott, you really need to think this through," Doc warned him. "My God, man! You've got six children. You're a grandfather! What are you thinking? What would Lucy do without you? Could you really just walk out on her?"

Scott looked at the ground. He looked at the sky. He fidgeted nervously in his chair. Then he looked straight into Wallace's eyes.

"I don't think I care. I just don't think I care anymore," he said as he choked back a nervous cough. He got out a handkerchief and blew his nose. He tapped his foot on the ground and stared off into space.

"I just don't know what to do."

"What you do is come to your senses, man!" Wallace blurted out. "How can you do that to your family?"

Scott had heard enough. He grabbed his hat and headed for the car. Doc yelled after him. He watched as Scott jumped in his car and headed off toward Mecca.

On December 13, 1912, Scott, who had divorced Lucy, married Stella. The couple moved away to Yardley, Washington, knowing they could not stay in Parke County. Albert, Frank and Wallace got together to discuss what to do. Elbert, Scott's eldest son was still around and working and would be able to help his mother. Lucy still had five children at home. Dayton Edward, who was eighteen, was working on the farm. Hazel and Adeline were teenagers and could help by taking in sewing and laundry after school. Raymond and Wallace were still very young. The Wheat brothers helped Lucy move to a home on Vine Street in Clinton where they could get a fresh start. Wallace was deeply disappointed in Scott, but there was little he could do about it.

Doc saw patients at the office almost anytime. They lined up early in the day to see him and often had to wait several hours. When it was finally his or her turn to go inside, the patient was greeted by a room packed with supplies. First, there was the buggy. If a child, Doc would invite you sit in it for just a minute while he took your photograph. Then it was time to hop out and follow him, past small wine barrels stacked around the room, into the examination room. When he had finished the exam, he would go into the medicine room to create a bottle of medicine for the patient, or, if the formula was complicated, he might tell the patient to come back in a few hours or the next day to pick up the medicine.

At the end of the day Doc would stuff all the dollars and change from his pockets into a mason jar. Some jars he filled with just gold or silver coins. When the jar was full he would hide it and start a new one. Sometimes he took a jar up to the orchard or somewhere around the family home to hide it. He buried so many over the years that he began to forget where he put them. Once he decided he would be smart and bury a jar of gold coins out on the sand bank in the middle of the Big Raccoon. Months later, a flood came and completely changed the location of the sand bank. He never found that jar again, much to his chagrin.

Doc would often walk to Rosedale to buy things that he couldn't get in Roseville. Edward Terry, a young man of eleven years, would often join him for the walk. His mother Isabelle, sometimes kept patients or did other work for Doc, and he enjoyed Edward's company. "Bud", as his friends called him, was a high spirited, imaginative youth who enjoyed the challenge of keeping up with the rapid walking pace of the energetic doctor. One of Doc's favorite snacks was peanuts. For every mile that they walked together Doc would give Bud one peanut to eat.

Bud picked corn for Doc on the farm in harvest season. He also worked in the coal mines helping drive the mules. He demonstrated for Doc his growing skills with the whip and how he learned to manage the cantankerous creatures. Doc gave him some riding lessons on his horses, and sometimes they would go for rides together on horse trails through the woods away from the roads filled with annoying cars.

Bud often accompanied him on herb gathering hikes. Doc took the opportunity to pass along some of his plant knowledge and love of natural things to the youngster. Several of the young people in the neighborhood earned money from Doc by helping him plant his garden or by caring for the cherry, apple and peach trees in the new orchard he had established on the hill behind the barn.

In 1915 an epidemic of pneumonia began sweeping the countryside. While pneumonia was always a difficult disease, more people became sicker from this strain and more died. Respiratory diseases were rampant. World War I was raging in Europe, but so far the United States had not been drawn into it. Despite the sinking of the British passenger ship, the Lusitania, that killed 128 Americans, President Wilson continued to try to keep the United States out of the conflict.

Eclectic medicine was under attack as well. The Carnegie Foundation for the Advancement of Teaching had published a paper entitled "Medical Education in the United States and Canada", popularly called the Flexner report after its author Abraham Flexner. The report had described the Eclectic college in Cincinnati as substandard to the requirements of a modern day medical school. The Eclectics were outraged at this slap at their training in what they felt was an effort by elite universities to take control of all medical training. The Flexner ratings put many independent schools in jeopardy.

Doc took some time away in September, long enough to attend the meeting of the National Eclectic Medical Association in Cincinnati because he had heard that John Uri Lloyd would be addressing the membership. Lloyd, who was constantly at battle with the trend of pharmaceuticals away from vegetable medicines, had made some exciting progress in his work in pharmacy, including the development of a cold distillation process for herbs that maintained even more of their fresh properties, a standard that both he and Doc believed was extremely important.

Lloyd stood on the platform and looked out over his physician associates. His words were both humble and forceful as he pleaded passionately in his quiet yet commanding manner for Eclectics to hold their ground in using natural remedies and to not fear the brand of "irregulars" that the mainstream medical community had placed upon them. He encouraged the young doctors to continue to study nature and to place what they learned above all else—prejudice, fads, criticism—and to consider the work that lay before them.

"Then let us each feel that we have a part to fill, a work to do, and the great cause of Eclecticism is to continue in the study of the preparation of plants," Lloyd said.

"I have largely excluded all else from my line of work. I have come to comprehend that all life action comes from vegetation, which I could not comprehend without the knowledge that was given to me by these men of the olden times. Whatever is in life comes from the plant; whatever acts on life beneficially, comes from the plant. And now, listen— you believed me when I taught you years ago and used a blackboard —let me tell you that all life structures that I know of, that all life foods that I know of, are colloidal, and colloidal chemistry is the chemistry in which we stop studying the molecules and study the action of structure on structure. We are walking colloids ourselves, every tissue of the body is colloidal, every food that we take is colloidal, and behind all the rest water—water, the material that, in the time to come, will be studied by the chemists and pathologists as the great source of functional activity in human plant being."

Everyone cheered! His rousing speech thrilled the members, and Doc left the meeting with a renewed sense of purpose.

By 1917 the respiratory epidemic was dying off but influenza seemed to be on the rise. On April 6th, the United States declared war on Germany after that country tried to recruit Mexico to enter into the world war, promising Mexico the chance to recover several U.S. states in the Southwest that were lost in the Mexican-American war seventy years before. This was too much to ignore, and even pacifist President Wilson was forced to take a stand. To Doc Wheat it seemed that the world had turned upon itself and was swallowing its population in evil and its resulting death and disease.

Fearful of an attack on the U.S. and the long distance it was to the nearest hospital, Doc decided that he should create an emergency treatment area. Down the hill from his father's house near the duck pond, Doc had men dig out a rather large underground area. It was supported by wooden beams and concrete blocks and was large enough to hold several small rooms. On one side of the entryway, he kept shelving where he stored jars and jars of tinctures that he was making to have an emergency supply. There were also several other rooms where he could see patients or use as hospital quarters. On the other side, there was an area set aside for a general work area. On the far back wall of cement blocks he had an American flag painted. He put big barn doors on the front of the dugout that could be fully opened in the summer to let in light and air.

It didn't take long for the dugout to get nicknamed "The Cave" by townsfolk. In the summertime Doc saw patients in the cave. It was much cooler for all. It was a much better place to keep many of his medicines and extra supplies. There was some natural light, but it had to be supplemented by lanterns or candles.

In 1918, an epidemic of Spanish flu began to ravage the world, and Parke County was no exception. The first wave hit in March, and most everyone who had fallen ill recovered after a couple of weeks. Then, an even more virulent second wave hit in the fall and a third wave in winter that took many lives. The influenza spread far more rapidly than past epidemics and in seasons when it was not expected. It also affected many young people from their teens to mid-thirties, a surprise to most doctors. Many died of secondary pneumonia. Dr. Wheat often discussed flu treatments with his colleagues. He preferred Aconite. DeElla Brown Joslin, who was now married and practicing in Terre Haute, Indiana, showed a preference for Gelsemium. Her mentors, the

Baldridge brothers preferred Bryonia. Macrotys, Veratrum, Eupatorium, Lobelia, Asclepias and Ipecac were other cures mentioned at state and national meetings.

This was not the usual age group affected by flu. It was normally the very young and the very old. Some thought it might be a version of swine flu, which was also running rampant through the animals and had been passed onto humans who worked with them. Some thought that birds might have passed it to humans. Doctors knew about what was called a virus, a very, very small and unseen disease-causing agent that some researchers said was the pathogen. No one really knew how to treat it beyond trying to make the patient comfortable.

Local doctors had their hands full tending to the many that had fallen ill and, also, in trying to educate the population, as best they could, about how to check the spread of disease. The flu was not the only disease they fought. Tuberculosis continued to ravage, and Albert's son Lawrence succumbed to it that year. Measles, mumps and scarlet fever were also high. Dr. Wheat tried to control fever with remedies like Aconite or Rhus Tox. He treated mumps with Phytolacca root.

It was all that Doc could do to keep up with the demands for his time. Many patients were too sick to come into the office, and he knew that it was better for the rest of his patients if these infected people stayed home. He made many a house call day and night by horse and buggy, or by car if one was available. There was little time to contemplate the causes and the meaning of it all. Doc was appalled at the thought that 10,000 young American men were being sent to Europe each day to fight. His nephew Dayton was among them. Doc had his hands full here at home.

The Great War ended with the armistice signed on November 11, 1918, and the men slowly began to return home from the European front, many bringing with them syphilis and other sexually transmitted diseases caught from prostitutes. These men also suffered from deep emotional scars of war. Doc saw many a veteran who found no outlet for the trauma he had suffered except through drinking or suicide. He did not know how to relieve their mental anguish.

P OKEWEED

(Phytolacca americana)

TWENTY

"Did you check along the creek? He could have fallen in and gotten washed downstream," Frank asked Wallace. The look of desperation his brother saw in his eyes made Wallace's heart sink.

His son Paul had disappeared. A young man in his twenties now, he didn't return from work in Rockville one day. He just vanished. Frank and Ann were frantic to find him. All their friends and neighbors searched the woods, the neighboring towns, the barns, the mines, and the creek beds.

"Yes, Frank, we did." Wallace told him. "No one found a trace of him. No one has heard anything about him or where he might have gone."

The whole family was devastated by the loss. Frank and Wallace spent the next few years searching every possible lead that was offered. Ann was a strong woman, and held up as best she could. She spent many hours in prayer for her child. The couple was deeply distressed, but there was little anyone could do.

Bud Terry left Coxville in 1919 to join the Texas 4th Cavalry patrolling the border with Mexico. At age seventeen, he figured what he had learned about mules might be useful to the military, and he thought it might be more steady work than the mines. Mine work could be irregular. Every day miners had to listen for the distinctive air whistle of the mine where they were employed. If it blew three times, that meant "no work today". At twenty-five cents a day, losing a day's wages was a hardship. He was right about the value of his skills to military service; the Army was happy to enlist a mule trainer. Bud wrote to Doc often describing what he was doing in the cavalry and about the new rope tricks he was learning.

The 18th Amendment to the Constitution prohibiting the manufacture and consumption of alcohol also passed that year and began to be enforced in 1920. Those in favor of temperance had finally won! While this didn't affect Roseville very much, already being in a dry county, it was the talk of the nation. Wallace and his brothers responded to the call for extra productivity from farmland to help with war recovery by planting corn and sorghum. They also heeded the call to tap some of their sugar maple trees to produce more syrup to help with the sugar shortage.

Doc remained active in the national and state Eclectic Medical Associations, but it was clear through news from the national school that the Eclectic Medical College was in trouble. The American Medical Association Council on Medical Education and the Association of American Medical Colleges had raised curricular standards requiring more laboratory facilities in schools and higher endowments for the support of the colleges in order for them to receive an "A" rating. Without this rating, the schools' students could not receive monetary support for their tuition.

EMI embarked on a two-year campaign to raise the needed funds, contacting all its alumni with a plea for donations and life insurance beneficiary pledges in order to build an endowment fund of half a million dollars. It was clear to most practicing Eclectic physicians that the school had not kept up with medicine's new focus on biochemistry and pathology. It lacked the laboratories to conduct needed research and it did not have a faculty that was adept at teaching new methodologies.

Back in Roseville, Doc was busy improving the way he made his own medicines. He installed large concrete vats in the orchard to catch rainwater, and he used this clean water for his medicinal preparations and for drinking. He was concerned about the amount of potential contamination of his preparations from well water. He needed a cleaner, purer source. He could distill fairly clean water from rainwater.

He also did some remodeling to the old house, adding a summer kitchen in the back and a longer porch that wrapped around the front of the house. He still lived in the office but spent time up at the other property. The remodeling made much needed work for some of the men in Roseville. Each year Doc held a Thanksgiving dinner celebration for his patients and friends. Every New Year's Day he held an annual gathering of everyone who worked on the farm to celebrate the usual bounty of the crops. Other family members frequently used the house when visiting or for family gatherings.

His practice continued to grow by word of mouth. Patients kept coming in ever increasing numbers. Cars lined up along Yankee Street as patients waited outside to see the doctor. It was not unusual to see license plates from Michigan, Illinois, Colorado and even California.

Patients park their cars along Yankee Street in Roseville.
Courtesy of Galloway Photo and the Parke County Historical Society

Some patients came from as far away as Great Britain and Switzerland to see the physician they had heard about from family or friend. People said he could cure what other doctors could not.

Doc had become very well known for his goiter cure. In addition to the shots he gave to the neck, Doc would also put goiter patients on a diet high in berries, especially raspberries, when they could be found in season. The raspberries were a pleasant anti-inflammatory for the body and a great source of fiber. Doc worked with Mr. and Mrs. Charles Cook, a local couple, who set up a ward in their home for all the cancer patients to stay while they took their treatment. They had a large house and set aside the main floor for the patients while they lived upstairs.

Doc would only treat surface cancers. He used a black salve with a primary ingredient of Bloodroot commonly used by physicians. He insisted that the patients stay through treatment so that the action of the paste could be carefully observed. He was never convinced that the treatment was totally safe. He kept a close eye on the affected areas as the cream worked to remove the cancerous cells fearing that it would continue to eat through good tissue.

Back behind Doc's horse barn, two neighborhood boys were digging for fishing worms one day, when they hit something hard. The boy who was shoveling thrust the shovel hard into the ground thinking that he must have hit a rock. Instead he heard the sound of shattering glass. Both boys began to dig and soon unearthed a shattered mason jar filled with hundred dollar bills. The bills had been carefully stacked together and rolled into a bundle that had been poked down into the jar.

The boys kept digging and soon found two other jars, each filled with silver coins. They took their newfound treasure home to their parents who didn't have much trouble figuring out who the money belonged to. Together the parents took their boys to Doc's office. They asked Doc if he was missing any money.

Doc looked at the families and the two boys and spoke gently, "Yes, I did have some jars of money that I buried when I was getting some construction done on the barn. I just lost track of it. Why?"

The boys held up a burlap sack for the doctor. He invited them all inside. When he opened the sack he saw the jars, and looked up at the boys and their parents.

"Where did you find this?" he asked.

"We were lookin' for worms back behind the barn, and we found these," one of the boys blurted out. "We're sorry. We didn't mean no harm."

Doc smiled at them. "I'm sure you didn't. And, I think it was right honest of you to take this money home to your folks." He stood up and shook the hands of the parents. "I appreciate your folks' honesty to return the money. There are many who wouldn't have done that."

"Doc, we knew it had to be yours," one father said. "We and our boys ain't thieves. None of us would ever want any harm to come to you."

Doc smiled. "Come on, boys!" He lifted each one up and put them in the buggy. "Now sit up nice there, so I can take your picture!" He got out his camera and snapped a nice picture of them together. Then, he gave them each a piece of fig candy and a quarter each as a reward for their honesty.

"Thank you all for comin' by!" Doc said as he waved goodbye to them. Everyone left in a happy mood. Doc took the sack of money back to his medicine bench. He picked the ceramic out of the paper bills and rolled them up inside a new jar.

Late that afternoon there was a bit of a chill in the air. It was a good time to walk. The cool air was exhilarating, and fall was turning into winter. Doc put on his hunting jacket and a pair of raccoon earmuffs. He really didn't like to wear a hat unless it was very cold. Earmuffs were enough! The hills were filled with the low and languid song of male crickets and katydids rubbing their wings together making music that almost sounded like a lament about the approach of the cold months.

As he gazed down into a ravine from a high ridge he could see the beautiful sycamore trees. Their white bark stood out against the darker oak and hickory trees. Even in the worst of times, the hills offered solace and serenity. Nature spoke a different language than man did. It whispered on the wind about patience and the timeless renewal of life at its own pace. It had no agenda, it just was. It had nothing to prove, it just moved on, cycle after cycle with a promise of more to come. It had no need to assert superiority, because, in the grand scheme of things it was far superior to anything that man had ever created. A man could take that with him from a walk in the woods and feed his soul. It was proof to Doc that something greater than we guided this whole crazy experience of life and that we were part of it.

The walk was just enough to wake him up and get his blood flowing as he started the evening's work of preparing the medical formulas for each of his patients. He started a small fire in the wood stove and put on a kettle of water to make some tea.

TWENTY-ONE

"There were some fine minds trained in that building, both spiritually and academically," Doc mused with Jacob Fisher as they looked at the smoldering ashes.

1925 seemed to be a year of shedding the old for the new. The old school house on Yankee Street where Doc's whole family had attended both school and church had burned to the ground. The community members met and agreed that despite the high expense it was time to move forward with a new school building that also had room for town meetings, banquets and other gatherings. A new brick school was planned and built up at the top of the hill in Coxville.

Scott's eldest son, Elbert Wheat, had agreed to take over management of the farm, and in exchange Doc agreed to have his family move into the big house. Elbert's wife Nellie and their children all helped work in the fields, tend to the animals and do the chores around the house and garden.

Doc had long wanted to be able to raise some of his own herb and medicinal plants. In early summer of 1925 he had a cement floor

New Coxville schoolhouse 1925. Courtesy of the Terre Haute Star-Tribune

poured next to the big house. It was the first stage of a greenhouse that would give him a place to expand his experiments with his plants, grow seedlings and work with grafting. He hired an engineer who helped him plan the building. They determined the needed dimensions, the type of glass and the glass framing he would need for the structure. To heat it, the engineer was devising a small steam power plant that would be built behind the house. It would connect to the greenhouse and the big house. The project kept him running back and forth between his office to see patients, the engineer's office in Rockville and the worksite to supervise the men. The cement would need time to cure before the large glass building could be constructed.

In July Albert agreed to stay at the office and greet patients who might come by while Doc took a much-needed vacation. Doc combined a trip to Detroit to a medical convention with a week of fishing and sailing on beautiful Lake Michigan.

Albert was reading a book when he heard a knock at the door. He opened the door and there stood three men who seemed a bit nervous.

"Doc Wheat?" a dark-haired, surly-looking man asked.

"No, Doc's not here," Albert told him. "He's on vacation.

"Oh," said the man. "Well, when do you reckon' he'll be back? We got to see him."

"Why? Are you sick?" Albert asked.

The man nodded and looked at the ground. His two companions stood there in silence.

"He should be back in about two weeks," Albert told them. "Can I tell him who you are? Are you already patients?"

"No. The name is Shively," said the man. "I'll just come back. Thank ya." The men left in an old Hudson automobile. Albert went back to reading his book and didn't think anymore about it.

Doc returned from his Michigan excursion relaxed and ready to get back to work. Many patients were awaiting his return, and the lines in front of his office were long the next day. The days of the following week were filled with work as he tried to get caught up. He enjoyed having Albert there to talk with and to share stories about his trip.

The next Monday Albert went to bed around 10 p.m. He slept on a cot that Doc set up for him in the treatment room. Doc was busy in his medicine room late into the night. Around 2 a.m. he heard a knock on the door. Not wanting Albert to be awakened, he rushed to the front door a bit perturbed that someone would come around this late. Of course, it might be a real emergency. He opened the door just a bit to see the same three men Albert had spoken with a couple weeks ago.

"Doc Wheat?" Shively asked.

Doc looked at the trio of men wondering why all of them had come to the door. He was immediately on his guard.

"Yes, what is it?" Doc replied a little gruffly.

"Doc, we come all the way down from Lafayette," Shively said. "My wife is awful sick with stomach complaints, and she says she knows you can help her. Can we get some medicine?"

Doc stared at the man for a moment. He was unsure whether or not to believe his story, but he decided it wasn't his job to be a judge of the man's character, just a doctor who helped heal.

"Good God, man! It's the middle of the night. I can make something up for you to take to her, but I have to have time to prepare it. How about if you come back in the morning, and I'll have it ready for you?" Doc asked.

Shively and Doc stared at one another for a moment as their eyes met. Shively stepped forward and put a foot in the door crack. He reached behind his back and pulled out a revolver, pointing it at Doc's head.

"How about you do more than that for us," Shively said gravely. The three men pushed their way into the office. They grabbed Doc by the arms. He was pulled into a chair and his arms were tied behind its back. The commotion woke Albert.

"What's going on? Who? Who are you? What do you want?" Albert said groggily as he roused from the cot. Then he recognized the face of the man who had come by earlier.

"You!" Albert yelled.

"Shut up," growled Shively. "Tie him up," he ordered. "One of the men easily overtook the older man. Soon Albert was gagged and tied face down to the cot.

"Leave him alone!" Doc commanded.

"Shut up!" Shively shouted and whacked Doc across the face with the revolver. The blow stunned Doc into silence.

"Just shut up and do what you're told, ya hear?" Shively threatened. One of the thieves was busy going through Albert's clothing looking for money.

"Ha, ha! Look, Joe! I done found twenty dollars!" the thief laughed.

"Leave him alone!" Doc yelled only to get whacked in the face again.

"Shut up before I break your jaw," Shively warned. "You're a pretty famous guy, you know, Doc? And, we heard that you ain't too fond of banks. That so?"

"That's preposterous! Let me go!" Doc moaned.

The thief slapped him with his hand again and again.

"There's talk that you got money buried around here, and if you'll just show us where it is, we'll be right happy to take it off your hands and git outta here," Shively responded with a grimaced smile on his unshaven face.

"I don't know who told you that," Doc groaned. "That's just a rumor. I don't have any money buried here."

"Well, that's just what I expected you'd say, Doc," Shively said. "I guess we're goin' to have to persuade you a little to tell us what we need to know." The thief untied his hands and pulled him up out of the chair and threw him on his back to the floor. One of the men took his arms, another man his legs and pulled them tight. The third man jumped knees first down onto Doc's chest. The blow knocked the breath out of him and he could feel his ribs crack. He gasped for breath.

"Come on, Doc. It ain't such a hard thing to do. Just tell us where the money is," cajoled the thief. "We got all night. I don't think nobody is going to hear us down here, and nobody is goin' to see us. The quicker you tell us where the money is, the easier it'll be on you."

"I tell you, I don't have any money here," Doc wheezed. "I'm telling you the truth."

Shively looked at him quietly for a moment. Then, he got down right in Doc's face.

"I don't believe you," said the thief, getting right up next to Doc's nose.

"Get him up," he ordered his companions. The other two men pulled him back up into the chair and tied his hands behind the chair back and bound his feet. Doc screamed from the pain only to get hit again above his right ear with the butt of the revolver. He worked hard at hiding his fear and tried to stay in command of the situation despite the pain he was feeling.

The men slapped him around some more, but it didn't get them anywhere. Then the man hit him across the face with the butt of his gun. Doc moaned in pain as his cheek opened up and began to bleed. He passed out. They threw water in his face, and he finally came around. The beating continued, but Doc didn't relent.

After about an hour of this the thieves went over to the corner and began to whisper. Finally, one of them went outside and returned with a miner's carbide lantern in his hand.

All three men came over to his chair. They untied Doc's hands from his back and then retied them in front. They cut a couple of lengths of rope and tied him all the way around the back of the chair. Then, they laid the chair backwards on the floor. Two of them removed his shoes and socks.

"Doc, I'm gonna give you one last chance to tell me where the money is. Then, if you don't, well, I think you can see what we're gonna do," the thief said holding the lamp in his hand. Doc just glared at them.

"I already told you," he gasped. "I don't have any money buried here. I got about fifty dollars in that jar on the shelf. That's all that I have." One of the thieves leaped up and retrieved the money from the jar.

"Well, that's good," said the main thief. "Now we're gittin' somewhere. Tell me where you got it buried outside!" he yelled.

"I tell you there isn't any!" Doc yelled.

"Wrong answer, Doc," the ringleader said. He stuffed a cloth in Doc's mouth as Doc began to yell.

Two of the men held Doc between them on the floor in the chair while the third lit the carbide lamp and began to burn the soles of Doc's feet with the burning hot little three inch flame it produced. Doc screamed out and writhed with pain as the thief slowly worked the lantern back and forth on the bottom of his feet. Over and over again, the men burned his feet trying to get him to talk. When they would remove the cloth from his mouth Doc could only scream with pain and repeat that there was no buried money, that he kept his money in a bank.

They burned the bottom of his feet for more than half an hour until they were totally black and holes had gone clear through to the top in a couple of places. The pain was excruciating, but still Doc did not relent. The thieves were getting very frustrated, still sure that there was treasure to be had if they kept up the torture long enough. At last they gave up on scorching his feet. They dragged him into the back room and sat him on the stove tying his hands behind the stove-pipe. They took coal oil and saturated his clothing with it.

"Look, Doc, this is your last chance!" Shively said as he got real close to Doc's face. "We heard that you got thirteen thousand dollars buried around here. Thirteen thousand dollars, Doc! That's a lot of money. And, if you want to live, you're gonna tell me where it is. If not, I'm gonna burn you alive!"

Doc was frightened out of his wits, barely conscious and nearly spent. Just then the train-crossing whistle suddenly sounded, loudly warning of an approaching train on the track that paralleled the office. Doc was exhausted and in great pain but managed to speak.

"You better get out of here," Doc blurted out. "The train always stops here right by the bridge. It'll be here any minute." It was a lie, but he hoped it would work because he could not hold out much longer.

Frustrated at their failure to break him, the men were still more fearful of being caught. The bell clanged loudly, unnerving the bandits.

"Come on, Joe, this ain't worth getting caught over", one of the thieves complained.

"All right. Come on. Let's git," a disappointed Shively called to his companions. They gave Doc one more whack to the face before they ran, leaving him tied on the stove. They fled out the front door, and Doc heard their car leave and drive down the road.

Doc eventually managed to yell for help. Among the first neighbors to arrive were Bill Cottrell and Joseph Wisher. Cottrell gasped when he saw the shape Doc was in.

"Doc, what happened?" he asked as he untied him from the stove.

"Bill, go check on Albert!" Doc replied weakly. Bill went to check on Albert who he found under a blanket bound but unharmed. Albert related to him what had happened, then went to get his nephew Bert to transport Doc to the hospital.

No one knew why the railroad bell suddenly went off that night. It simply malfunctioned. There was no train coming. Some called it a miracle, because if it hadn't been for that strange occurrence Doc would likely have lost his life. As it was, he was severely injured and in greater peril than he might have suspected.

(Arnica montana)

TWENTY-TWO

"Do you think he will ever practice again?" Margaret asked Albert.

Although filled with doubts himself, Albert didn't let on that he shared her concerns.

"Of course he will! He's very strong," he assured her. He looked toward his brother, lying in bed. The wounds were dreadful. He knew the beating that his brother had taken. He felt guilty for being unable to help as he heard him tortured. Now, the least he could do was to take care of him. He knew this would not be an easy time for his brother. To be so completely dependent on others would go against the grain.

Word eventually spread about Doc's torture and beating. More people around Parke County might have heard what happened to him sooner, had it not been for a major fire in Rockville the same night caused by an exploding gasoline water heater. The fire burned down seven buildings in just forty minutes. The whole town was focused on the disaster.

Doc was not the best of patients. He stayed in the Terre Haute hospital only long enough for them to treat his ribs and head, just a few days. He insisted they use his own remedies on his burns, water soaks infused with Calendula or Comfrey. He had the wounds dressed with honey and Calendula to help prevent infection, as well as taking Echinacea to boost the immune system. He also had his bruises treated with a Comfrey root poultice. The family was told that he would be off his feet for an undetermined length of time. It could be months, and the wounds would have to be watched carefully and cared for daily. The family members gathered together and tried to figure out how could help. Patients would have to be told. They would notify those they could find. Out-of-town patients who showed up would be very disappointed. Doc would need around-the-clock care for awhile. All the family members offered their time to cover his needs.

Albert and Margaret set up a bedroom for Doc in their home in North Terre Haute where he could be cared for more easily. Margaret was deeply worried about him. At first Doc refused to see anyone except close family members. He detested the idea of well-wishers coming by, certain that their intentions were more to spy on him and to have new fodder for their gossip than to encourage his return to good health. He would listen to no allopathic physician about his treatment and continued to direct his own care. He fought his own depressive moods, making him a genuinely cantankerous and unpleasant patient, driving everyone to the point of wishing they could send him home.

His endless determination to not be an invalid soon set in. Less than a month after his beating Doc put a personal notice in the *Rockville Tribune* notifying his patients that he was open for business to anyone willing to travel to Albert's home to be seen. This did not please Margaret, who resented Doc using her home as an office. She complained to Albert, but he reasoned with her that this was something Doc really needed to keep moving forward with his recovery.

While his bruises and cuts healed, his injured feet kept Doc disabled for many months. Fear of infection was a constant worry. Doc needed every ounce of his strength of will to deal with the intense pain. He tired quickly and took only a very small amount of morphine when the pain was more than he could tolerate. His frustration level was high, and, for the first time in his life, he was considering his own mortality and wondering if he would be disabled for the rest of his life. At age fifty-five his recuperative powers weren't what they used to be. Still, he fought back, sometimes hour by hour, against his own fears. His beliefs were being put to the test that the body could heal itself if certain conditions of aid were met.

DeElla Brown Joslin came to the aid of her old friend. She was able to help in ways that others couldn't. He trusted her; he trusted her medicine; and they had a special bond from those days in medical school so many years ago and as colleagues in medical practice. She visited him on a regular basis to check and dress his wounds and listen to his advice on his own treatment. She was a sounding board for his complaints and had a way of calming his fears and bringing him peace of mind. She even helped him formulate medicine for patients from her own stock.

"DeElla, I don't make a very good patient," he told her. DeElla laughed.

"That, my dear friend, is the understatement of the year!" she teased him. "I'm certain that you will make it through this trial. Absolutely certain of it! I'm not so certain about the rest of us! You need to quell your tongue a bit. It is so unlike you. Remember that everyone is making sacrifices to help you. At least try to be a little patient and a little less demanding. Everyone will be so much happier."

Doc scrunched his nose at her and gave a little smile. He knew she was right. He had been miserable toward those who loved him the most.

"It has been quite a journey, hasn't it? This medicine we practice."

DeElla looked at him, a bit amused.

"It has indeed. I often think back to those medical school days. I didn't find much acceptance among my colleagues then, and, except for you and a few very good friends, I don't find much now. I have not been able to practice the full range of medicine I am capable of, but, I've managed to secure a place for myself primarily taking care of women and children," she said.

Doc looked at his friend. She was still good looking even with gray hair and wrinkling skin. Her eyes still sparkled and her spirit seemed undaunted.

"You didn't give up," Doc recalled. "I always admired that about you. Men can be cads!"

"Some men," she said as she bandaged his feet, "but not all. I remember one who was quite my champion years ago and gave me the strength to go on by standing by our friendship. You ran the risk of alienating practically the whole student body before you had even started your studies. That was a very brave thing to do. I have been eternally grateful, and it helped the other women in the class as well."

Doc looked at his friend. He could only imagine the things she must have faced from some of his less polite and more egotistical colleagues who considered the medical profession the last place that a woman should attempt to be.

"You have been a good doctor, and a good friend," he assured her. She gave him a small dose of morphine and soon he fell asleep. Her presence helped him relax and rest.

Recovery took far longer than Doc had hoped but not longer than he had imagined for someone his age. He was too knowledgeable to be fooled by anyone about the nature and gravity of his condition. Even DeElla did not paint a rosy picture for him. Still there was something intangible in the strength of his will to recover that kept him going through the toughest times.

Elbert managed most of Doc's affairs in Roseville while he healed, and Doc was very grateful to him. His young family pitched in and put up food for the winter months, cared for the animals and maintained the property.

As Doc struggled to recover, the world of the Eclectic medicine faced continuing struggles. The brand placed upon them as practitioners of "irregular" medicine had caused some of their graduates to drop the name Eclectic from their practice for fear of being ostracized by fellow doctors in their local medical communities.

A campaign to alumni to raise the needed funds to keep the Cincinnati institute viable had failed to raise enough cash to sustain it. In 1926,

Dean Thomas chose to suspend the entrance of a new freshman class. He told alumni that he feared a total collapse of the school by the time the current sophomore class graduated if needed funds could not be raised. He once again called upon all who considered their school their medical home to give generously to keep the doors open. In addition to giving money, Wallace wrote letters to his fellow Eclectic physicians encouraging them to support the school. He would have preferred to do even more if he had the strength.

It was nearly three years before Wallace was able to return to Roseville. He endured painful exercises each day to try to rehabilitate himself. He made very slow progress for the wounds were so deep that too much flex in the tissue would cause bleeding or seepage of fluid. He would try to stand upright every day, although he was often unsuccessful. He was confined to a wheelchair for a long time.

In the interim the thieves had been caught, tried and sent to prison. Doc had insisted upon attending the trial, so Albert took him to the courthouse in his wheelchair where he gave testimony for the prosecutor and publicly admonished lawmakers for not having harsher punishments for the perpetrators of such crimes.

Doc finally was able to walk on crutches, then with two canes. He was able to tolerate being on his feet for short periods of time. In the spring of 1928 he decided that it was time to go home. He was anxious to be useful once again. His family decided that moving home was the best thing for him to do. They took turns checking on him daily. Elbert's wife, Nellie, was able to bring him his meals. He began seeing patients on a limited basis. He plunged into practice with all the strength he could muster. He convinced everyone he was fine.

Doc's greenhouse project had been long delayed by his injuries. Now it was time to finish it. He immediately hired men to carry out the plans that were drawn earlier. The greenhouse ran the length of the south side of the big house. He supervised construction of the building with its whitewashed wooden frame. The men carefully installed the many glass windows. People from three counties drove to Roseville to see it.

Tired of waiting for rural electricity, Doc solved his own needs. He had the planned steam furnace added behind the house. The furnace room was the height of a one-story building and ran on water piped in from Big Raccoon Creek. The chimney was the tallest structure on the property and loomed high over the back of the house. It provided heat and light for both the house and the greenhouse. He even had a tunnel dug to the cave hospital and had electricity strung down there for all the rooms.

Doc soon filled the greenhouse with herbs, medicinal plants and vegetable seedlings. He was like a child with a very large new toy. He was constantly smiling when he was in the greenhouse. It was both his botanical laboratory and his place to escape the world. It was filled with the scent of fragrant leaves and delicate flowers and fresh, dark soil. It was almost as good as a trip to the woods, which he dearly missed, now that walking was such a chore. In winter it became his heaven on earth, and he often rested there. It was much warmer than his office. He would put his bedding on the ground in the center of the room. He felt comforted there, and, much as it had been when he was a child, he could communicate with the plants in a way that he couldn't with his fellow man.

The plants responded to his constant attention and meticulous care. He created fertilizer for them from fish caught in the creek. He developed a system of watering by poking holes in a rubber hose and snaking it down among the pots so many could be watered at once. He even grew lemon trees and fig trees. To him, there was nothing as good as a fresh fig!

In winter the windows were covered with moist droplets from the steam in contrast to the frost-painted crystal pictures in the corners of the windows of the big house. It was a place to think, to plan, to dream and to create. He began planting seeds in late winter so that by spring there were vegetable plants to set out in the garden. He could have greens all year round with staggered plantings.

His nieces and nephews dug and prepared the outdoor vegetable garden. Onions, garlic and peas were planted first, then potatoes. Next, green beans, squash and pumpkins were planted. Finally the tender plants, tomatoes, peppers, and herbs would be set out after all danger

Dr. Wheat's family home and greenhouse. Courtesy of the Terre Haute Star-Tribune

of frost had passed. Everyone knew that Doc would share the bounty of his garden with his friends and neighbors. He fed his chickens and ducks with grains but also with fruit and vegetable scraps. They laid large eggs with bright, golden yolks. Wild geese often stopped along the creek and were welcomed to the pond. Life was getting back to normal.

The stock market crash of 1929 sent the whole country reeling. It took some time for the devastating effect of the country's economic depression to reach Roseville, but it soon took hold. Some small banks failed with depositors losing all their money. Larger, more stable banks began to call in loans they had made. Suddenly, farmers and businessmen who had been able to borrow nine dollars for every dollar they had on deposit were faced with demand for payment of their entire loan. Many businesses closed. Farmers who needed good crop prices to pay back the banks saw the price of commodities drop until even their production costs could not be recovered. Many farmers went into bankruptcy, and their farms were put up for sale. The mines began to lay off workers as the price of coal plummeted, and some shut down completely.

Doc worked as hard as he could muster through it all. His strength slowly returned and his mobility increased. He had gained weight during his time of disability. Exercise had to take a form other than walking. He could walk just a little better each day, but he could not tolerate riding a horse. He would wear big boots and pad his feet with cloths to cushion them when he walked. It took a lot of mental fortitude to manage the pain that he continued to feel in his feet and legs from the nerve damage done by the injuries.

In late 1930, Elbert Wheat contracted pneumonia, which became worse as each month passed. By July 1931 he was bedfast, and he died just before Christmas. Nellie still had young children to raise. Doc assured her that she and the children could stay in the big house. To make more money, Nellie took over the stand down by the bridge that Sally used to run to sell coffee and sandwiches to the patients waiting to see Doc. Young Bert, Elbert's eldest son, took over management of the farm and property.

The Depression years were hard for all, but Doc's medical practice still brought in many patients. He would see all who came. People wandered up and down the street waiting their turn. In winter they would huddle inside the local stores. The Kinsey's set up a small store in the living room of their home and sold some food and general items. Some people would become impatient with waiting and try to bump up their place in line in a disorderly fashion. Doc was getting tired of solving disputes. He offered Nellie's children a chance to make money by creating an orderly line. Millie, Mary Alice and Junior took turns selling tickets for ten cents to buy a place in line. This soon solved the problem of line cutting and provided the family with some much needed additional income.

As the Depression continued to worsen, Doc's brother, Frank, who had been in failing health, died in August 1932. He never solved the mystery of his eldest son's disappearance. Some thought he might have died as much from a broken heart as from a disease.

TWENTY-THREE

Doc didn't spend much money on himself, and he didn't give many gifts. He didn't mind paying someone for goods or labor. He would honor friends, neighbors and workers with parties. Each year he invited patients and friends to the big house for a Thanksgiving dinner of turkey and wild duck. In mid-summer he might have an ice cream social on the front lawn.

It was mid-afternoon on July 25th, 1933, when guests began to gather. The Chicago World's Fair was the talk of people all over the Midwest. Young Bert Wheat came back from a visit to the fair with wonderful stories about the amazing things that he had seen. In honor of the fair's theme, and in keeping with the nature of today's celebration Doc called the dinner party "A Century of Progress".

Today's gathering was a special, double celebration. It honored what would have been his father Lee Wheat's one-hundredth birthday, and it was also brother Albert's seventieth birthday. Albert and Margaret Wheat and younger brother Lee, Jr., who all now resided in Kansas City, had driven back to Roseville to be there for the celebration. Doc had invited seventy-five friends and relatives.

A fire lit in the early morning had created a bed of glowing coals. A very large kettle filled with water had been placed on the fire and heated to boiling. Twenty-five plucked and gutted ducks were dropped into the steaming water. Soon they would be cooked to perfection. Several long tables were set up in the front yard and covered with layers of butcher paper. No plates or cutlery were provided for the guests; however, napkins were in plentiful supply.

"Ladies and gents, please gather round!" Doc yelled out. "Please, may I have your attention!" Everyone gathered in a big circle as Doc began to speak.

"Dear family members, special friends and guests, welcome to a very special day of celebration for the Wheat family! It has been one hundred years since the birth of Edward Leander Wheat, my father and the father of my brothers Albert and Lee, Jr. who are with us today. He is the father of Scott and Dayton who live in the Western states and could not be here. He is also the father of Horace, who left us some time ago, of Frank, who recently left us, and several other siblings whose time on earth was very short, rest their souls.

"Many of you are the fruit of his vine, the fine wine of his vintage, and he would have been most proud of every one of you. He was a most generous man. He took his sister's children upon her death and raised them as his own. He took his boisterous brood of seven boys and kept us all together as a family after the death of our beloved mother, Margaret Ann. He was a man of fortitude, vigor, patience and perseverance! He was a fine merchant, a successful farmer, postmaster for our community, a diligent township trustee, and, above all, a loving father. We miss his wit, his wisdom and his council. We are gathered here today to pay homage to him, to our lineage and to the fine lives we lead because of those in our family who came before us. If you have a glass, please raise it now in toast. If you don't, find one!"

Everyone laughed and found a cup for the toast.

"To the kith and kin of Edward Leander Wheat! May the family enjoy many wonderful years together!"

"Here, here!" Everyone responded by raising their glass toward the doctor and then to one another.

"Now," Doc continued, "we have someone else who deserves our recognition and who enjoys the celebration of seventy years on this earth today. My older brother, Albert, has been the backbone of our family. He became a second father to all his brothers when our mother died. Manhood was thrust upon him at an early age, and he met his responsibilities most nobly. Albert has been a store clerk, a farmer, a merchant, a businessman, our county Auditor, and a reliable employee for a number of firms throughout his life. In fact, I found the 'Colonel', as I call him, pretty hard to keep up with," Doc added with a chuckle.

Everyone nodded and buzzed with approval at his remarks.

"Albert, you have the undying gratitude of the brothers you guided through their youth, and the respect of every man and woman here. May your seventieth birthday be the happiest yet, and may you have many more to come. Happy Birthday!"

"Happy Birthday!" everyone chimed in and all raised their glass to Albert who raised his in return.

"Many thanks!" shouted Albert. "Now, come on, Wallace; we're all hungry!"

"All right, all right!" Doc said. "Let me explain the dinner plan. One hundred years ago our parents were born. In the 1830s no one ate with utensils. No one thought there was anything better than these hands!"

Everyone laughed.

"One hundred years ago they did not use knives or forks, so neither will we! Your first course this afternoon will be wild duck, pulled from the bone at these tables. There is meat, bread and pickles along with some fine sauces. Make yourself a sandwich. Plenty of napkins here, too.

"For our second course, some of our most elderly guests and the brothers will gather inside the house for a table dinner. Here we will eat like we did seventy years ago in honor of Albert. Over yonder will be a fine spread of fruit, bread cheese, potatoes, tomatoes, and many other things...complete with plates, knives and forks. The third course will be our favorite dessert of modern times, cake and ice cream, so leave some room for that. Enjoy yourselves!"

Special guests at Dr. Wheat's Century of Progress Dinner. Left front are
Albert Wheat and Lee Wheat, Jr. Right front are Dr. Wheat and Jacob Fisher.
Courtesy of Galloway Photo

The hungry feasters began to line up at the food tables. Several
women had volunteered to tear apart the wild ducks and cut bread
for the guests. After finishing the first course, eleven men and one
woman broke away and gathered at the living room table in the house.
Mr. and Mrs. Cook, who tended to Doc's cancer patients, joined the
three brothers; Mr. Cook's father, who was nearly a hundred years old
himself; Nellie Wheat's father, Sam Ogborn; and four cousins from
Elbert Wheat's family. The long table was covered with butcher paper
and the food was presented in big, communal trays. Fruit, boiled
potatoes, green beans and venison were shared.

The final course of the feast looked like a celebration of light.
Torches were lit around the yard, as the light of day began to fade.
Everyone gathered in a circle around a table in the front yard as two
cakes ablaze with candles came around the corner from the summer
kitchen. One cake had one hundred candles; the other had seventy.

"Oh, my!" Albert cried out. "You don't expect me to blow out all of those, do you?"

"I expect you to try, Colonel!" Doc laughed. "Come on! Try!"

"You can do it!" everyone called out with encouragement. Albert took as big a breath as he could muster and began to blow. The young nieces and nephews rushed to his aid and helped him blow out the candles. Everyone cheered!

"Cake for everyone! Ice cream, too!" yelled Doc. "Help yourselves."

The youngsters screamed with delight. The grown-ups clapped.

As the sun began to disappear from view, a few of the guests began to depart, many walking through the dim light of dusk to homes nearby. Others piled into automobiles and drove off to neighboring towns. Many would spend the night here. Some pitched tents in the front yard. Others would stay in the house. They sat in chairs or on logs or lay in the grass and continued to enjoy the evening as night fell. Someone brought out a guitar, another a fiddle; still another pulled out a banjo, and someone else a dulcimer. Soon they were all playing familiar songs while people sang along or told stories between tunes. It was a wholly pleasant day.

(*Primula veris*)

TWENTY-FOUR

Prohibition ended in December 1933. Many hailed the end of the era that had created more destruction than preservation of people. It became clear that banning alcohol only created greater problems with people sick from rotting livers, brought on by alcohol poisoning from the consumption of homemade moonshine. It killed many. Organized crime had gained control of liquor sales. Some other solution to the alcohol problem had to be found.

Lobbyists pushed for repeal of the Eighteenth Amendment, citing the need to weaken organized crime. They proposed controlled liquor sales with taxes levied to raise much needed revenues. Congress complied, repealing the amendment to the Constitution and allowing each state to determine its own liquor laws. Indiana created the Alcoholic Beverage Commission to oversee and enforce liquor sales and licensing.

Doc agreed with the change. He welcomed the change in the law for the general public. He had treated many a patient with alcohol poisoning. There was only so much one could do for a damaged liver. He treated them with goldenseal root tincture. It not only helped the liver, but it also was an appetite stimulant and helped with digestion.

Dr. Wheat in his sixties. Courtesy of Galloway Photo

Many of the alcoholics suffered from malnutrition from improper eating habits. He might encourage them to drink Dandelion Root tea since a mild bitter could help the appetite. He might also give some Milk Thistle tincture for jaundice or liver congestion. He would never condemn a patient for their choices in life or blame them for an illness. Still, he had always failed to understand a person's need to put the poison of alcohol into the body, except for the small amounts used in medicine. He could never make them understand its effect on the body; they just didn't care to know. He never hesitated to mention the need to stop drinking to his patients, no matter how often the advice was ignored.

Doc's physical condition was much improved, but it was still difficult for him to walk. He no longer wanted to live so isolated from the family in the big house, and he wanted a better office for his patients. He had another slab of concrete poured behind the house and construction began on a long, thin building made of yellow tile block. The building had ten small rooms and a small waiting area for patients. It was a quite plain, functional building with no frills. Doc moved in, abandoning his office by the creek after twenty-seven years.

Doc finally retired the old buggy to the barn. When he moved it up there, he remembered that he had put several jars of money up in the loft. He went up to retrieve the jars thinking they would now be safer in the blockhouse. To his chagrin he found that mice had somehow found a way into those jars and had shred the money to bits.

He connected the new building to the steam heating system. He used one room as his bedroom, one as sleeping quarters for young Bert, and another as a guest bedroom. One room was a small laboratory and another was the medicine room where he kept his bottles of tinctures and his money. The rest of the rooms were used to see and treat patients. He was pleased with the change. His accommodations were more comfortable now, and he enjoyed being near the family and especially the greenhouse.

The building of the blockhouse was a project that kept a number of men in the community employed throughout the summer. Doc gave it close supervision as he would any project. Ever-patient Nellie kept the men fed with sandwiches and delivered Doc his dinner each night. He never ate with the family. She closed the stand down by the bridge. There wasn't much need for it anymore. Fewer patients came these days. The family had been greatly inconvenienced by the disruptive project, but Nellie never complained. Doc had helped support her family all these years. Why shouldn't he have more comfortable quarters of his own?

In 1934 Doc was elected president of the Indiana Eclectic Medical Association. The Eclectic movement faced many challenges, and all the Eclectic medical colleges except EMI (now called the Eclectic Medical

College of Cincinnati) had closed their doors as universities took over the training of doctors. Drug companies had endowed medical schools with research and scholarship funds. Such support gave universities the upper hand in determining the future of medical practice.

Chemistry had greatly advanced the manufacture of drugs that were more easily controlled substances than were plant-based tinctures and cheaper to produce. Dosage could be standardized and results measured without the difficulties faced using plant extracts. The work of the Eclectics to create medical treatments from native material medica and their specific formulas were now ignored. Still, the school's administration and some alumni tried to keep the medical movement viable.

The Eclectic Medical College, after a period of falling enrollment and discord among the faculty, had pulled itself together and modernized its facilities. They were turning out qualified doctors, but the number of practicing Eclectic physicians had now fallen to only about six thousand. Despite advances in medicine and the rise of germ theory, the Eclectics stuck to their conviction that plant-based medicine was the only medicine truly fit for human consumption. They continued to believe that the life force of plants helped the human body heal itself from its infirmities. From this point-of-view there was no backing down.

As association president, Doc had his work cut out for him communicating with other Indiana Eclectic physicians. He tried to get them to vigorously participate in the state association. He encouraged them to write papers for presentation at state meetings. He traveled the state talking with as many of the membership as he could. He encouraged them to share their knowledge with other association members.

He traveled to Indianapolis that spring for the annual meeting. As president he would address the association. He bought a new suit and decided to treat himself to a visit to the hotel barbershop. He had a manicure, shoe shine, shave and a haircut, and felt like a new man!

On May twenty-second, he addressed the annual gathering of the association at the Hotel Lincoln in Indianapolis. His speech bemoaned the attitudes that he found among his fellow physicians:

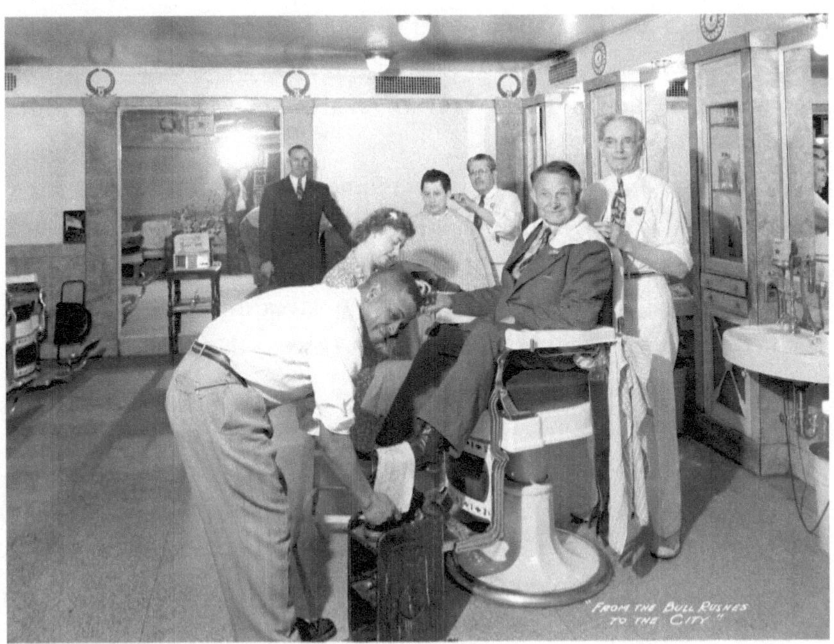

Dr. Wheat gets a makeover. Courtesy of Galloway Photo

"Within the past half century I have heard the addresses of several of the Presidents of our nation; I have heard the addresses of presidents of different organizations; I have even heard the address of the president of a fox hunters' association. And many of these have made the statement that 'there never was a time in our history when we need a more thoughtful, more courageous and more economical action than now.

"As this was true in the past, so it is true today. As we sat and listened to our teachers and professors impart this truth to our brains, too often did it pass through without absorption. When the tide changes, and we are placed in their positions, then, only then, do we realize.

"About thirty years ago, just across the street in the assembly room of the Claypool Hotel, there was a great gathering of Eclectics, and their friends, and the room was filled to overflowing. Many crowded about the door to gain entrance. The program was excellent, and the story of the hobgoblins was recited {by Mr. James Whitcomb Riley}. Since that time, there have been many times I thought the hobgoblins had me, but, being on the alert, I managed to get by. And even in the face of death, when the angels were flitting around my brain, I relied on the good old-fashioned remedies, and here I am seemingly younger than I was thirty years ago.

"Now the present is with us, and under the [Mr. Roosevelt's] 'new deal' no one knows positively whether the little hole in the table will get the proceeds or those who labor diligently and sincerely will be rewarded, too. I wonder if the one who saves ninety percent of his pneumonia patients will be rewarded the same as those who save forty percent.

"At the present time, as in the past, there are two main forces at work among human souls. First, there is the force of destroying the human body, as in the case of war, when people are shot, shocked and shelled for the deliberate purpose of destruction, and some risk their own lives for the destruction of others. Second, there is the force of saving humanity—people who risk their own lives to save others. The sincere physician is an example of one who is trying to save others, even at the risk of his own life. I pause for a moment. (All bowed their heads in a moment of silent meditation.)

"With all the human bodies that are killed by war, fire, flood, droughts, disease and pestilence, still some survive. And when we look around us and read and see the number that have gone and the number that are here, we are led to the thought, 'Oh death, where is thy sting? O grave, where is thy victory?'"

He thought about his professors, those who had guided the Eclectic school through rough times, as he said,

"The Scudders, Kings, Wintermute, Watkins, Freeman, Bloyer and Thomas have passed on and their families have felt the sting of death, and their graves have been a victor for their bodies, but their cause lives on in the hearts of those who knew them. The cause of trying to save a human life is still with us, and may it continue forever. The means for saving life lies with each individual physician, and in proportion as he selects the right remedy to overcome the cause of death, in that proportion is he successful.

"Now, as to the Indiana Eclectic Medical Association. If our association is to live on, it must have supporters in its work. The more supporters we have the larger the association. It seems that one of the greatest troubles the officer of this association has is to receive favorable answers to letters sent out to physicians. In canvassing the state for papers, I think I have found out one of the greatest obstacles in the association work.

"According to a prominent Indianapolis physician, he is unable to see why Eclectics try to join other societies and take little interest in their own. He says further that Eclecticism is nothing to be ashamed of. In answer to this, I think I have found out one of the main reasons for this. In approaching a prominent Terre Haute physician for a paper, he looked sort of cock-eyed at me and said: 'There is some work to writing a paper, is there not?' I said yes. Said he:

"'I have quit work, so will not write a paper.' Now, gentlemen, this is your trouble. When we all quit work, this association is gone, and with it the rest of us.

"If we should all stick to the motto 'Labor Omnia Vincit,' we shall conquer our troubles and survive longer and be happier. As to the future of Eclecticism! We shall see it survive in proportion to the labor put in it. When the Eclectic colleges of the United States went down, it seemed to have a depressive effect on the physicians. But now that the parent college in Cincinnati is running nicely, it should give a better hope for the future."

He pulled a small paper from his pocket and began to recite a poem:

When the Depression is over, and things get true,
And the times get better, and the finance too,
And things not handled for just a little few,
We'll have a better feeling for the red, white and blue.

His words were spoken in the true spirit of determination to help the Eclectic approach to medicine survive. Yet, so much change was occurring in medicine that the Eclectic doctors and medical students generally ignored his plea. New discoveries were coming rapidly as technology opened new doors for medical investigation. Money, politics and the desire of physicians to elevate their profession to new heights of prominence and recognition fought against the idealism of the hard-working country doctor. Medicine was on track to administer to the masses, to find cures and solutions that solved the health problems of the many, not the individual.

Doc understood where the medical changes were leading, and he could not argue that helping more people was a good thing. Still, his personal conviction held that medicine needed to keep in mind that each person was an individual with their own physical profile. He would never be convinced that mass medicine would be as good as his treatment tailored to the one patient.

After the meeting had adjourned Wallace was in the lobby of the busy hotel discussing a few items with his colleagues, when he happened to look up. As he scanned the lobby he noticed a beautifully dressed woman standing on the other side of the room staring at him. Her eyes looked so familiar, and her smile. The hair was gray now, but the beautiful face was unmistakable.

Doc excused himself and started walking toward her. He wanted to be sure that he wasn't just imagining her standing there. She watched him approach. Doc came close and his heart nearly stopped.

"Is it really you?" Doc managed to say.

Louise blushed. Her first impulses were to take his hand or give him a hug, but she restrained herself, uncertain how he might respond.

"Wallace," she started with a bit of hesitation. "It has been a long time. What are you doing in Indianapolis?"

Doc was so busy looking at her that he scarcely heard her words. Finally, he spoke, "I'm here for a medical convention. And you?"

"I live here now, I had met a friend for lunch here at the hotel." They both stood there awkwardly for a moment.

"Would you walk with me?" Wallace asked. "It really is good to see you."

Louise consented. She took his arm, and they walked and chatted, eventually working their way out to the small rose garden at the back of the hotel. They sat in the perfumed air among the flowers on a white wrought iron bench catching up on the years. Wallace felt the surge of love he had known once before when he was in her presence. He at once desired and feared to ask the question of why she had left him. He was too much of a gentleman to broach the subject.

Nor did it take Louise long to feel the strong attraction to Wallace that she had felt so many years before. She related to him how she had gone home, and then, to Indianapolis to work in a private school. Through her contacts there she met and eventually married a prominent businessman. She never had children.

Wallace listened with interest to her, and then told her only the good things that had happened to him over the years. Both approached the meeting with maturity, leaving any animosity and other strong emotions out of the conversation. The years had given them the opportunity to control their feelings, to see each other, and to part as friends.

Doc watched Louise as she bid him good-bye and once again walked out of his life. She had found the fulfillment that she needed, he thought. Likely, she would not have been happy as the wife of a country doctor who spent most of his time occupied with things other than her. Just seeing her again was healing to the wound she had left, one much harder to heal than those holes in his feet. Still, he found that he could love her in spite of her decision, and he respected her for making a choice that must have been difficult, but, in the end, was the right choice for her.

Louise didn't look back after she left Wallace. She couldn't. She still thought him among the most noble souls she had ever met. Their meeting had stirred her to her core, and it would be many days before she would forget seeing that sincere and loving, albeit eccentric, man again. She, to this day, had silently thanked him for not pursuing her and complicating her decision.

After his year at the helm of the Indiana Eclectic Medical Association, Doc completed his presidency and returned to Roseville. He was finished trying to convince other Eclectics of the worth of their own method of medical practice and discouraged that so few saw the value of the fight. His patients were fewer in number now, and he began to spend more time grafting plants and enjoying time with neighbors and friends.

TWENTY-FIVE

By the winter of 1938 Bert Wheat was having severe back problems. It became apparent that he could no longer effectively run the farm. His sister Mildred was graduating from high school and was moving away. Nellie's family decided that they would give up the farm work and the house and move to Rosedale. It was quite a change for Doc to no longer have the family around. He had lived quite humbly all these sixty-eight years in order to accommodate living quarters for the family. The big house stood empty. Doc had no desire to move into it. He hired a housekeeper to look after it, and relatives or guests stayed there when they visited. Babe Cottrell took over supervision of the farm.

In Europe, German leader Adolph Hitler transformed his country into an armed state unfriendly to Jews and many other ethnic groups. Many fled. By fall, war in Europe seemed unavoidable, and people across the United States feared being dragged into the conflict.

Doc received a letter from Bud Terry, whom he had kept in correspondence with him over the years. After a short stint in the military Bud had changed his professional name to Tex Terry and had become an entertainer on the Vaudeville circuit doing a roping act. He wrote:

Dear Doc,

I guess learning to herd those mules at the coal mines with the sound of a whip turned out to be a pretty good thing. Who would have ever guessed that I could make a living showing people whip and rope tricks! After some years on the road with my act I have landed in Hollywood, California. I have gotten some small roles in the movies, and I think I might be able to find steady work here. I just played a role in a Gene Autry film called "Rovin' Tumbleweeds". Autry liked my looks to be a bad guy. I think that is a role I could take on for these singing cowboys. He also likes my leatherwork. I'm working on a new saddle for Autry now. Say "hello" to the folks at home for me.

Best wishes,
Bud

The whole idea of movies excited Doc. Always an avid photographer, making pictures of people actually moving set his mind in motion. He purchased a movie camera as soon as he found one and started shooting footage of family and friends. He held movie nights in the big house so everyone could see his little films. It was thrilling for all to see themselves on screen.

Life did not change quickly in Roseville, but, in the larger world, medicine was making great strides forward. Powerful microscopes now helped researchers see levels of life that had not been seen before helping them to understand the causes of disease and to develop new treatments. The approach to medicine that the Eclectics had chosen to defend had lost the approval of the majority of the medical community. In 1937 the first sulfanilamide came on the market with amazing curative results against some of the most difficult diseases caused by streptococcal and staphylococcal infections. The Food, Drug and Cosmetic Act of 1938 set out new standards for safety in commercial pharmaceutical production.

The Eclectic Medical College had reorganized and reopened its doors for a freshman class in 1931, but the American Medical Association continued to list the practice of Eclectic medicine as 'extinct'. This meant that students at the college were unable to get loans to pay for their education. The final freshman class was taken in 1936. It graduated its last class of thirty-six doctors at Memorial Hall in Cincinnati on June 9, 1939.

The medical profession had shaped itself through the first half of the twentieth century into a profession that had stringent requirements for a student to secure a license to practice. Many doctors took additional training and became specialists in only one area of medicine. Young doctors were no longer inclined to return to rural areas where they would make much less money. Some of the potential medical students who might have been persuaded to return to their local communities couldn't afford the cost of the degree.

Doc was given no rest as the world changed around him. He was still the only doctor in Roseville. People still came to him for his personal method of attention and his herbal cures were still effective.

The attack at Pearl Harbor on December 7, 1941, dragged the United States into the massive world conflict. New drugs were being developed at a rapid pace as universities and pharmaceutical manufacturers worked feverishly to find treatments to meet the needs of war. The mass manufacture of the new antibiotic called penicillin saved the lives of thousands of soldiers and civilians. Soon other new antibiotics followed. The whole face of medicine changed from the use of botanicals to chemotherapeutic drugs, and the prescription synthetic drug became the standard.

Pharmaceutical companies rapidly abandoned making botanical tinctures for the more powerful and effective new drugs that promised high profits for their companies. The old 'shotgun' approach of herbal medicine that offered general assistance to the human body was replaced by the 'silver bullet' treatment that targeted specific symptoms of the illness. No one could argue with their effectiveness, not even Doc, although he never felt that they were the best thing for the human body.

Throughout the war years the newspaper published photos of the many young men and some women who were drafted or volunteered to join the armed forces. Doc was filled with remorse. He knew many of them. He had helped deliver quite a few of them into this crazy world. Now their chances of survival were questionable. What a great tragedy, he thought, that so many fine young people must fight a war put upon them by those too old to fight themselves. He grieved for their sacrifice.

Doc worked hard during the war years foregoing all thoughts of retirement and continuing to practice. So many of the young doctors had gone into the service that those physicians left behind carried an equal burden. Each year he held a Thanksgiving celebration for patients and friends at his home. Nellie helped organize the gatherings and recruited other neighborhood women to help cook and serve the meal. Doc hired a bookkeeper, Mrs. Mary Elkins of Paris, Illinois. She came at least twice a week and was sometimes an overnight guest when there was sufficient work to be done.

At last the war ended and thousands of young men and women began to return home from what had been the most mechanized war in history with its deadly consequences. It had ended with the deployment of the new and devastatingly destructive atomic bomb dropped on Hiroshima and Nagasaki, Japan. It was a more terrible weapon than most could have ever imagined, and Doc was heartsick over what his country's leaders had chosen to end disputes.

Doc's practice began to dwindle as other physicians returned home from service and resumed their practices. Fewer young people brought their children to him since the idea of using herbs as medicine was not very modern and not the way that they had been introduced to medical care. Dr. Wheat began to be talked about as the eccentric old guy who still used old-fashioned medicine. His reputation for hiding money in mason jars stuck to him like glue although few people bothered him at this point. He was a bit of a legend even in his own time, and many thought he was a recluse who didn't really like people.

One day, a youngster named Charles James was brought to his office by his parents. Charles was suffering from blood poisoning. According to his father, the doctors had given up on trying to cure him and gave him just months to live. The couple was desperate to save their child. Even though they considered coming to the old herb doctor a last resort, they were grateful that Doc thought he could help. The treatment for septicemia was slow and steady, with a special diet and Echinacea tincture with a few drops of Baptisia for the purplish hue of the mucous membranes. It helped the body cleanse itself of the poisons. After a few months Charles had fully recovered.

TWENTY-SIX

By 1947 many soldiers had been discharged from the service and were flocking home in great numbers. It would take years for society to settle back into a routine after the world war. No one's life would ever be the same. The men came back to meet children they had never seen. If they were lucky, they had a wife who waited for them and kept their family intact. Many relationships broke up when the soldier who had seen so much could not readjust to civilian life. Now the battle was psychological as men tried to deal with what they had experienced. Few spoke of what they had been through. Many things were broken—lives, people's spirits, and, for some, their moral compass. Doc hired some of them to help on the farm and work in the greenhouse. He knew that contact with living things would be beneficial to their frame of mind. The peaceful country setting of Parke County offered a restful atmosphere away from the sounds of war.

Glenn Fisher and Sam Gregg were Coxville teenagers, and Doc gave them work to do around his property. Glenn's father ran a general store down the road at the bottom of Coxville Hill. Sam was Doc's neighbor Sally Gregg's grandson. Sam had spent a good deal of his life being raised by his grandmother. His mother, Sally's daughter, Nellie May, was a bit of a wild seed, first running away to become a circus performer that rode the Hell on Wheels walls atop a motorcycle. She was a pretty woman who had a string of marriages.

Nellie May Gregg and baby Sam. *Courtesy of Wanda Miceli*

She had become pregnant by a man who had ended up in prison before they could marry. Nellie May then married someone else. Doc had known about the pregnancy and had helped Nellie May with the birth of the child and then gave her some money. When Sam was with his grandmother, Doc took an interest in him and tried to act a bit like a surrogate father. Sam never quite understood the relationship or why Doc paid so much attention to him, and resisted what Doc tried to do, thinking of him more as an adult who was trying to run his life, rather than as an ally. As teenage boys do, he sometimes resented Doc's interference in his affairs.

The boys had been assigned the task of cleaning up the inside of the barn, cleaning out the horse stalls and straightening up the gear. They had just about finished a particularly messy corner when Sam spied a large milk can that was sealed and shoved way back under a pile of boards.

"Glenn, look," Sam said as he pointed to the can.

"Yeah, it's a can...so what?" Glenn said in a sarcastic tone of voice.

Sam pulled some of the boards off and laid them along the wall of the barn. He tried to pick up the can, but it was fairly heavy. He tried to open it, but the can was sealed shut.

"What do you suppose is in there?" Sam questioned as he tried to break the seal.

"What do you care?" Glenn responded. "Come on, we got work to do." Sam put the can back in the corner, and the two took their load of used hay out to the compost heap. But, Sam didn't forget about that can.

Later in the evening, he came back. No one was around. Sam looked up and down the road. He didn't see a soul. He went in the barn, found a crow bar and carefully pried the lid off the milk can. What he saw inside made him gasp. The can was filled to the brim with money—silver coins on the bottom, which was why it was so heavy, and hundreds of one dollar bills filling about three-fourths of the can. He grabbed a burlap bag and filled it with all the paper money. He resealed the can and put it back in the corner. He sneaked out the back of the barn and took the money to his own secret hiding place. Later that year, Sam went to visit a friend in Kentucky. He was drinking with her and her boyfriend, Oran Arthur, and he began to brag about the little "job" he'd pulled, how easy it had been.

"I couldn't believe it when I opened that milk can, how much money there was!" he told them. "I guess the old man just doesn't like banks; that's what I hear."

"You mean he just leaves his money sittin' around like that?" asked Oran.

"Yeah. I reckon he gets robbed pretty regular," Sam said. "Every once in awhile I see someone show up about his place with a shovel, and he will come out and shoo them off. I don't think he ever even missed that money I took."

Oran took it all in with great interest. It wasn't long before the men had hatched a plot to relieve Doc of some additional wealth. Sam gave Oran the information he needed about Doc's habits and when he would most likely be away from the office.

On the first Tuesday in November, Doc left with Charlie Brown for Terre Haute early in the day, as he always did on Tuesdays. Four men pulled their car off the road within walking distance of the house and watched until everyone was gone. They took a walk down to the creek and pretended that they were interested in something down there.

When they were certain no one was around, they walked down the creek bank and up to the back of the house and entered Doc's office by breaking a window and unlocking the door. It didn't take them long to find the money room and clean it out. A search of the rest of the building didn't yield any additional money. They loosened a few floorboards on the porch of the big house but didn't find anything more. They started toward the barn, but soon saw that someone was in it tending to the horses. Not wanting to stay too long, and fearful that someone would see them, they headed back toward the creek and quickly circled back to the car.

Walter and Roy Arthur, Oran's brothers, and Ollie Lowe laughed all the way to Rosedale about how easy it had been to come in and rob the old man. They headed south through Rosedale where an alert town marshal, Toney Apfel, noticed them stopped alongside County Line Road. Walter was smearing mud on the car's Kentucky license plate. Suspicious of their presence in Indiana, he quickly wrote down the license number and called Sheriff Botts, who put out an alert to Terre Haute authorities to be on the lookout for the car.

Harold Roseberry, a state detective, spotted the car heading toward North Terre Haute and pulled it over. He questioned the men about who they were and what they were doing in Indiana. He reached into the car and opened the glove compartment to retrieve registration papers. Instead, he pulled out a whopping handful of paper money. When Walter Arthur saw this he quickly opened the car door and rammed it into Roseberry knocking him to the ground.

As he fell, Roseberry saw Ollie jump out of the rear seat and reach for his pistol. With lightning reflexes, Roseberry pulled his gun and shot at Ollie three times from the ground, hitting him twice. A passing police squad car saw the incident taking place and stopped just in time to take the men into custody. Ollie Lowe was taken to the hospital with a bullet in his stomach and under his arm. Roseberry fractured two vertebrae in the scuffle.

The four men were arrested for auto banditry and were initially held in the Vigo County jail. When Sam Gregg heard where they were, he went to the jail to visit the four. He told the officer that he was there to retrieve the car from the Arthur brothers who had promised it to him. Sam was taken into custody as the "finger man" who had helped the four set up the robbery.

Thanksgiving dinner 1947. Courtesy of Galloway Photo

Doc with dinner guests Thanksgiving 1947. Courtesy of Galloway Photo

TWENTY-SEVEN

On Thanksgiving 1947, Doc organized a big dinner at his home for his friends and patients to celebrate the end of World War II. Everyone was dressed in their Sunday best. The serving tables were loaded with good food including Doc's hand raised wild ducks, root vegetables, bread, cranberry salad, pudding, cake, pie and ice cream. Doc served as master of ceremonies.

"It gives me great pleasure to have all of you—my friends, associates, and my patients, here for a very special Thanksgiving! We thought the first World War was the war to end all wars. Who would have ever thought that we could rise up in conflict against one another in such a terrible, and highly mechanized way as we have done for the past four years. I truly thought that the world had gone mad! I offer a moment of silence for those who lost their lives in this conflict."

Everyone bowed their heads to remember the dead and wounded.

"But, now, all that is behind us, and our country survived and stood strong! It took the effort of us all to make this happen. Tonight, I salute you for whatever small or large part you played in this war.

It was important that each one of us acted like patriots and did our duty. The alternative to victory was too horrifying to allow. Let us hope that the world will come to its senses and never allow such an all-consuming conflict to happen again!

"Now, I have a confession to make. It is not normally my habit to eat two pieces of pie....but tonight I did! One apple and one cherry. And I enjoyed every bite! Ladies, our hats are off to you for tonight's wonderful meal. Thank you!"

Everyone laughed and applauded. They were grateful for his generosity to the community and presented him with a nice engraved pen and pencil set. Frank Miller led a toast to the good doctor. Several local children sang a song, and a local musician played a classical

An elderly Dr. Wheat on a winter's day. Courtesy of Galloway Photo

composition on the violin. The evening ended with a moving picture show of Doc's travels last summer in Texas and Mexico.

Winter soon closed its icy hand on Parke County with frigid temperatures and heavy snows. In mid-February, Walter Arthur, the only man who did not plead guilty to the robbery, was put on trial. The courtroom in Rockville was packed with police officers, witnesses and the curious. Upper classmen from the high school were excused from classes for the day so they could attend the proceedings. Teachers thought it to be a great real-life class assignment. No case in the county had ever involved such a large amount of money! Some people wanted to view the evidence just so they could see what forty-two hundred dollars in cash looked like.

It only took one hour of deliberation for the jury to find Arthur guilty. Judge Hancock sentenced him to ten years in prison. Sam Gregg had been charged with grand larceny and had also received a ten-year sentence for his part in the robbery.

Doc had gone home after the trial and tried to put it all behind him. It had been a strain on him at age seventy-seven to be part of such a public event and to have to sit on the hard courtroom benches. His arthritis was bad in all his joints now and, especially bad, in his feet. He was in constant pain but too stubborn to let anyone know it. He had learned how to keep a smile on his face no matter what difficulties he encountered. It was the best way to maintain his privacy.

About a month later, there was a knock on the office door. Doc yelled from the medicine room for whoever it was to come in. Two men entered the waiting room. They were wearing suits.

"Yes, what is it?" Doc asked.

"Doctor Wheat, I'm Randall Cogburn and this is Gerald Mason from the Internal Revenue Service," the man began.

"What do you want?" Doc asked.

"Well, Doctor Wheat, our office heard about the robbery to your office and about the large amount of money presented at the trial. We've been asking around about you, and you seem to have quite a reputation for hiding your money here and there."

"I suppose that's true," Doc said. "Why?"

"The IRS has some questions about your income…whether you have been reporting it all. I'm here to inform you that we intend to audit your tax returns. I wanted to give you time to gather the needed information and prepare. We're going to need to see your patient payment records, your receipts and expenses to determine if you have been paying enough in taxes."

After the men left Doc sat down in a chair. He did keep better records than he used to. He had hired Mary Elkins several years ago to set up his accounts. He would consult with her about what he had to do. He had never imagined having to go through an audit, and he was distressed about what it all meant and what the consequences might be. He went over to Paris the next weekend to visit at the Elkins home and to discuss with Mary what he should do. Mary promised to help him sort things out as best she could for returns over the past seven years.

It was midday, and the weather was hot the third week of August in 1948. Doc walked slowly home from the greenhouse to his office, thinking about having a bite of lunch. He was feeling a bit strange. His chest felt tight, and, as he walked, he felt short of breath. He entered the blockhouse and started toward the money room. A pain gripped him in the chest and he fell to his knees, holding his hand over his heart. He lay down on the floor, closed his eyes and just rested. So many thoughts raced through his head, he quickly diagnosed his condition. His only strategy was not to move, and he lay there for some time trying to figure out what to do next, how to get some help. Mrs. Elkins found him a couple of hours later and put him to bed.

Doc had not improved after a couple of days and Mrs. Elkins encouraged him to let her take him to her home where she and her husband could care for him. They loaded him into their car and took him to their home in Paris, Illinois. Doc was adamant that he would be all right, although he knew this was not the truth. After a week with no improvement, Mrs. Elkins phoned Albert in Terre Haute. Lee, Jr. was also notified and came from Kansas City.

The three brothers chatted quietly in the bedroom.

"Colonel, I want you to look after my affairs when this is over," Doc whispered to his brother. Albert looked at him. He had never thought he would outlive his younger brother; but, from Doc's pallid complexion he realized it would be true.

"Of course I will. Don't worry," Albert reassured him. Lee looked on with quiet resolution. One or the other of the brothers, or the Elkins, stayed with Doc day and night until the end came a few days later on August 31st with a final heart attack.

Wallace W. Wheat was buried on a warm, bright September day. The sky was soft blue hue, and fair weather clouds drifted by on a warm breeze. Dozens of cars lined the streets by the cemetery in Rosedale reminiscent of the days when they lined up along Yankee Street in Roseville waiting to see the doctor. Many more people showed up on foot tramping through the short grass to the back of the graveyard to the Wheat family's gray-stoned plot. Almost all the residents of Roseville/Coxville came to pay their last respects. Many carried a roadside flower or a small herb to put on the grave. They stood with Dr. Wheat's medical colleagues and with patients and friends from across the state that came to wish the good doctor goodbye. Historian Charles Roll had included him in his book, *Indiana: 150 Years of American Development* (1931) as one of Indiana's most prominent citizens.

Although Doc had not attended church very often in adult life, his family insisted on a Christian ceremony. The doctor would not have objected. While he did not really practice religion, he believed that life was run by something higher than mankind. He believed that doctors should be heroes and should put their lives on the line for their patients, if that is what it took.

The mourners with eyes fixed on the ground stood silent, as the minister prayed and blessed the passing soul. His words penetrated their thoughts and brought to mind for each the memories they held of the doctor, a man with both a fervent zest for living and deeply held convictions that made his own path undauntedly clear to him. Some stood there that day because he had refused to give up on saving their lives. He was their hero. Now, what would they do? Who would they turn to for healing? How could they replace the only doctor in town? They never did.

In the first few weeks following his death, Nellie and Bert Wheat stayed at the big house. They had to keep a shotgun near the door. Word had spread about Doc's death as had the freshly spun tales of how he had buried money all over the property. After all, had it not recently been all over the news? Many people thought it was just fine to come over now with their shovels and dig around for those money jars. They came in broad daylight. They snuck in at night. They broke windows in the greenhouse trying to get in. They dug under the porch and around the foundation of the house and the barn. They dug up the whole yard. They pulled boards off the side of the house and dug up the garden. The family had their hands full chasing people away.

Was there really any money there? Yes. A woman who later lived in the house had a dream about money being hidden in the greenhouse. She found several hundred dollars when she checked the location. One day the hogs routed up several jars of money from the mud. Louis Treep, who bought the house, found several jars of money out by the trash pile. The bills were scorched but salvageable. He turned the money over to Doc's family. In all, he found about seventeen thousand dollars. Even as late as the early 1950s people were still coming around and trying to dig for money.

Mr. Treep worked for the area DuPont factory. When the plant shut down, he was unable to sell the house. The county repossessed it for delinquent taxes. The dugout cave where Doc had his emergency hospital was eventually filled in with dirt after being declared a safety hazard. The house, blockhouse and greenhouse have all been torn down.

The Roseville bridge still stands.

Bud "Tex" Terry had a fifty-year long career in Hollywood as a working actor in Westerns playing the villainous bad guy for cowboy stars Roy Rogers, Hoot Gibson, Gary Cooper, and Gene Autry. He played his first movie role in 1924 where he used his whip in *Don Juan* starring Douglas Fairbanks. An artist in leatherwork, he made leather items for many of the Hollywood stars of the era, including many belts and holsters for John Wayne.

Isabell Drazmere was his agent. She had guided the careers of Buddy Ebsen, Hugh O'Brian and Vic Tayback and had discovered young Indiana talent James Dean. Isabell and Tex later married. They moved to Parke County after Tex retired from acting. They first tried to start a business venture called Frontier City in Mansfield that failed. Later they opened the Longhorn Tavern in Coxville with a Western

Tex Terry with his Cowboy Cadillac in front of movie studio, Hollywood.
Courtesy of Tex Terry website, www.texterry.com

theme that celebrated Tex's movie career. He entertained at many area schools and social events with his rope tricks. He died in 1985 and was buried in the Coxville cemetery.

Today there is only one business in Coxville/Roseville. The Rock Run Café remains in the building that housed the Longhorn Tavern. All the other buildings are gone, and only a few residences remain. Yankee Street is now known as Coxville Road. No doctor has practiced in Roseville since Dr. Wheat.

Mordecai "Three-Finger" Brown went on to play professional

Mordecai Brown.
Courtesy of the Mordecai Brown Legacy Foundation

baseball leading the Chicago Cubs to World Series victories in both 1907 and 1908. The spin he could put on the ball caused batters to hit it into grounders, quickly scooped up by the Tinkers to Evers to Chance infield. He spent much of his career with the Cubs, but he also played a single season for each the St. Louis Cardinals and Cincinnati Reds. Brown also played and managed in the short-lived Federal League for St. Louis, Brooklyn, and Chicago. He ended his major league career in 1916, but continued playing and managing for minor league teams, college squads, and specialized semi-pro barnstorming clubs well into his later years. When he completed his baseball career, he returned to Parke County as a business owner within the Texaco Corporation, all the while keeping active in his passion for hunting, fishing , and, of course, baseball. Mordecai Brown passed away at the age of 71 in 1948.

Doc's brother, Dayton Wheat, died in 1949 in Great Falls, Montana. Lee, Jr. worked as a Red Cap in Kansas City for many years. Albert lived to be ninety years old and remained the stalwart head of the family.

While this book has focused on the life of one man, there were many others who made Coxville/Roseville a village of distinction. Their contributions were not less than Dr. Wheat's. A community is built on the work and contributions of many fine people.

In 1915, the Coca-Cola Company held a competition for a bottle design for their soda product. They wanted a bottle so distinctive that even a blind customer could recognize it as a bottle of Coca-Cola. The Root Glass Company of Terre Haute decided to enter the competition. Company president Chapman J. Root; plant superintendent Alexander Samuelson; auditor E. Clyde Edwards; secretary Roy Hurt; mold shop supervisor Earl R. Dean and William R. Root, son of the president went to work on the project. Edwards and Dean found a line drawing of a cocoa bean pod, and, from this, Dean developed a bottle design with a bulging middle and parallel grooves with tapered ends. The name 'Coca-Cola' encircled the bottle. Sand from the Roseville Acme Glass Sand Company was used for the project. Elements in the glass gave the bottle its unique green tint.

The design won the competition. The bottle was patented under

The 1915 prize-winning Coca-Cola bottle. Courtesy of the Vigo County Historical Society

the name of Alexander Samuelson in November of that year. The Root Glass Company held the bottle patent and received a five cent per gross royalty until 1937 when Coca-Cola acquired the rights. The 'contour bottle' or 'hobble skirt bottle', as it is also known, is now a registered trademark of Coca-Cola. It has been called the most recognizable container in the history of the world.

The stories, innuendo and reputation of Doctor Wheat have, over the years, made him into a Parke County legend and folk hero. There are still a few people alive who knew him personally. He was just a man who applied himself to his profession and to his life in the community. His impact was deeply felt by those who had the privilege to know him. It is unfortunate that no medical notes about his treatments have survived for the benefit of those who have an interest in natural medicine today.

Eclectic Medicine and Today's Naturopathic Approach

The work of the Eclectic medical movement has not been lost. King's Dispensatory remains an important record of the power of natural medicine and the importance of plants in the healing process. Today's naturopathic approach to medicine has underpinnings in the pioneering work of the Eclectics.

Edward Alstat, a naturopathic physician and the pharmacist for the Portland Naturopathic Clinic, and Michael Ancharski, a naturopathic physician and Clinic Director for the National College of Naturopathic Medicine, founded The Eclectic Institute in Portland, Oregon, in 1982. Their purpose was to create a line of botanical medicines that met the high standards of purity and freshness required for their clinical work.

They developed a line of botanical products using only organic herbs harvested and processed while fresh. They re-published several of the Eclectic medical books along with modern commentary on treatments and pharmaceuticals, and published modern naturopathic texts. They have re-introduced the work of Eclectic physicians to modern-day naturopathic physicians. Dr. Ancharski later left the business, and Dr. Alstat moved the operation to a larger farming and production location in Sandy, Oregon.

For more information visit their website: www.eclecticherb.com

Lloyd Library

The Lloyd Library and Museum in Cincinnati, Ohio, holds the complete papers and history of the Eclectic Medical Institute and has become a repository of many books and papers on botanical medicine, alchemy and botany. Scholars from around the world come there to learn from those who went before them and to better understand plant-based medicine.

For more information visit their website www.lloydlibrary.org.

A Partial Genealogy of the Wheat Family of Parke County

Ruth Wheat Boatman, Edna Wheat Calvert, and Mabel Wheat,
with two other women.
Photo by Wallace W.. Wheat Courtesy of Galloway Photo

Generation 1
John Wheat, Jr.
married Mary A. Noland

Generation 2
John Mulliken Wheat
married Miriam M. Berry
        Children: Caroline Lavinia
                           Benjamin Dyer
                           Edward Leander (Lee)

Generation 3
Caroline Lavinia
married Harman Henry Hagar
        Children: Lizzie
                           Edward

Benjamin Dyer
married Elvira Francis Ferguson
        Children: None

Edward Leander
married Margaret Ann Nail
            Children: Fred (died in infancy)
                                 John (no dates listed)
                                 Albert (7/25/1863 – 5/4/1954)
                                 Frank (1/8/1865 – 8/21/1932)
                                 Twins (1866 not named, lived 3 wks.)
                                 Horace (10/1868 – 10/4/1888)
                                 Wallace (6/5/1870 – 8/31/1948)
                                 Scott Wheat (4/13/1872 – 3/19/1951)
                                 Dayton (3/20/1874 – 2/15/1949)
                                 Lee, Jr. (12/3/1875 – 2/19/1962)
                                 Daughter (3/17/1877
                                 died at birth, never named)
married Adaline Cox 10/19/1890

GENERATION 4

Fred Wheat (5/7/1862 – 3/19/1877)
John Wheat (no dates listed)
Albert Wheat (7/25/1863 – 5/4/1954)
married Margaret Isabell Neilson
            Children: Elizabeth Edna
                                 Clarence
                                 Lawrence W.
                                 Ernest Albert
                                 Ruth Dell
                                 Mabel Marie

Frank Wheat (1/8/1865-8/21/1932)
married Ann Craig (no information)
            Children: Paul B.
                                 Edward
                                 Mayme
                                 Icie
                                 Oressa
Twins (1866, not named, lived 3 weeks)

Horace Wheat (10/1868 – 10/4/1888)
married Dora King
Scott Wheat (4/13/1872 – 3/19/1951)
married Sarah M. Lucy Edmonds (12/11/1870 – 2/24/1946)
            Children: Elbert Ervin
                                 Dayton Edward
                                 Hazel
                                 Adeline
                                 Raymond
                                 Wallace
married Stella Carell (circa 1889 – ?   ) in 12/13/1912

Children: Virginia
                   Margaret
                   Donald R.
Wallace W. Wheat (6/5/1870 – 8/31/1948)
Dayton W. Wheat (3/20/1874 – 2/15/1949)
married Della Turpin (6/18/1876 – 7/1968)
          Children: Crystal B.

Lee, Jr. (12/3/1875 – 2/19/1962)
married Verna Zell Wheat (circa 1888 – 10/17/1938))
          Children: Lee, Jr.
                             Jack Norman
married Cora Edith Fairchild (12/26/1885 –6/3/1974)
          Children: Daughter (3/17/1877 died at birth un
                             named)

GENERATION 5 (PARTIAL)
     Elbert Ervin Wheat (12/9/1890 – 12/1931)
     married Nellie Ogborn (12/11/1894 – 11/1984)
          Children: Bertram
                             Mildred
                             Mary Alice
                             Junior
                             James
                             Billy Ben
                             Wayne

Acknowledgments

My thanks to many friends and colleagues for their help and encouragement. A special thanks to the residents of Roseville/Coxville, Indiana, for sharing their stories and their memories of Dr. Wheat. My research was rewarded by the work of many Parke County historians and social news writers who have put facts and stories to print in magazines, journals and area newspapers, including The Rockville Republican, The Rockville Tribune, The Daily Clintonian, The Terre Haute Star-Tribune, The Paris (Ill.) Beacon-News, Parke County Times and Progressive Country Life magazines, and Parke Place Magazine, so richly documenting the lives and events of the area.

A special thanks to Mildred Wheat Bland, great-niece of Dr. Wallace Wheat, whose memories of him added new dimensions to his story. Her family occupied the Wheat family home for many years during Dr. Wheat's life while her father, Elbert Wheat, supervised the operation of the Wheat family farm.

A special thank you to Chuck and Jan Galloway, whose Wheat family photo collection offered a visual record for this story. Chuck is the grandson of Albert Wheat and Dr. Wheat's great nephew.

My thanks to the following:

John S. Haller, Jr. Emeritus Professor of History and Medical Humanities, Southern Illinois University Carbondale. His research and scholarly writings on the Eclectic medical movement were essential in to my research. He served as a great source of information and encouragement.

Charles Mark Bee, Imaging Technology Group, Beckman Institute, University of Illinois, offered his expertise and generous assistance in selecting photographs and illustrations, including long hours improving the quality of some very old photographic imagery. He also created images of medical bottles and tools that were incorporated into the cover design.

James Nardi, Ph.D., Life Sciences, University of Illinois at Urbana, and a native of Parke County, Indiana, offered both his knowledge of the flora and fauna of the area and his childhood recollections of Roseville. Jim was responsible for choosing the illustrations for each chapter that were important botanical sources of medication for Dr. Wheat and the Eclectics.

Edward Alstat, R. Ph., N.D., co-founder of the Eclectic Institute, Sandy, Oregon, who first broadened my understanding of the Eclectic medical movement. His efforts to preserve the medical information of the Eclectics and his continuing work on botanical preparations have been instrumental in keeping them available to modern day naturopathic physicians.

Dr. Francis Brinker, Clinical Assistant Professor, Department of Medicine, University of Arizona College of Medicine, and consultant to the Eclectic Institute for his review of medical treatments mentioned in this book and his contributions to my understanding of Eclectic medical practice and the use of botanical preparations and treatments.

Steven Foster, who guided me to critical resources, and was a source of great encouragement.

Wanda Miceli, who shared the story of her father Sam Gregg and the Gregg family.

Doris Rose Cottrell Nebergall who shared the story of her birth.

I would like to thank the staff of the Lloyd Library and Museum in Cincinnati, Ohio, for their assistance, especially Alex Herrlein, and for their willingness to use excerpts from their collections. Excerpts include portions of Dr. Wheat's presentations to the Indiana Eclectic Medical Association 1904-06, his address to the association as their president in 1934, and an excerpt from a speech by John Uri Lloyd to the National Eclectic Medical Association in 1915.

Karin Woodson, docent of the Parke County Historical Museum and native of Rosevlle, who spent many hours with me searching through documents, introducing me to residents and taking me to important sites.

The assistance of Lynn Lee, Parke County Public Library; Mike Lewman, Parke County Historical Society; Jean Gosebrink, St. Louis Public Library; Edgar County (Illinois) Historical Society; Jason Stratman, Missouri Historical Society; Teresa Pennington, Paris Public

Library; Mara Hayne, Vigo County Historical Society; Kacy Allgood, Indiana University School of Medicine Library; Linda Butler, DePauw University Library; and the Indiana State Library are deeply appreciated.

Thanks to Scott Brown and the Mordecai Brown Legacy Foundation for the use of photos and for providing historical information. Thanks to Ted Osborn of the Tex Terry website for a photograph and information about the career of Tex Terry.

Editing assistance also was provided by Michael Valentino.

Some of the many others who have contributed to this effort include:

Dennis Abernathy, Geraldine Barnett, Glenda Brewer, Sharon Calvert, Doyne Carson, Jerry Chaney, Galen Clavio, Katie Metz Clavio, Glenn Fisher, Olivia Clavio Fleming, Da'ine Greene, Shirley Lowe Heiman, Lynn Holland, Joe Hyatte, Alice and Tom Hyatte, Christina Jaeger, Sheri Johnson, Carl Jones, Charles Jones, Michael Kelsey, Nan McEntire, Pauline McKinney, Barbara Wheat Palmer, Nancy Stodart, David Tamulevich, Jim and Pam Virostko, and Wallace Wayne Wheat.

Finally, a special thanks to Ed and Karen Lauterbach whose encouragement first prompted me to move forward with this project.

Laura Z. Clavio.

Laura Z Clavio is a writer from West Lafayette, Indiana. She is a graduate of Indiana University and has worked as a television and radio personality, newspaper reporter, conference planner, and performing arts presenter. She is a native of Clinton, Indiana, in Vermillion County, and grew up just a few miles from where Dr. Wheat practiced. She first became familiar with Dr. Wheat when working as a newspaper reporter and feature writer covering Parke County.

9 781888 483178